Lonely is the Knight

A Merriweather Sisters Time Travel Novel
Book 3

Cynthia Luhrs

This book is a work of fiction. Names, characters, places, and incidents either are products of the author's imagination or are used fictitiously.

Lonely is the Knight, A Merriweather Sisters Time Travel Novel

The soul is here for its own joy. Quote from Rumi

Acknowledgments

Thanks to my fabulous editor, Arran at Editing720

May each and every one of you find your very own
knight in shining armor.

Chapter One

Prologue

Present Day—Deep in the Carpathian Mountains

Charlotte woke coughing. Smoke filled the room and she could see flames. The tiny wooden building was on fire. She couldn't believe it. The man who'd tried to kill Melinda, put her in a coma, was dead. This was a simple accident, nothing more.

She was deep in the Carpathian Mountains, where she'd run to get away from all the craziness. On her hands and knees, Charlotte crawled for the door. It wouldn't open. Something was blocking it from the other side. She grabbed one of the scarves Lucy had made her and held it to her mouth to keep the smoke from filling her lungs. As she crawled in the opposite direction, she searched for the window. It was her only way out.

The sound of a raven calling came from her left. The bird

seemed to be leading her to safety. Charlotte pushed up the window and rolled over the edge, landing in the snow. She breathed in, coughing, her battered lungs burning.

Charlotte sat in the internet cafe and checked her email. Her friend Jake was housesitting and said the police were trying to get in touch with her. When she called, the nice officer informed her Melinda had taken her own life.

Even though she knew there was no way both of her sisters had tried to kill themselves, Charlotte let the tears fall. She knew in her heart there was no way both of them had fallen to their deaths. But she didn't say any of this to the officer. She thanked him for telling her and ended the call, sniffling and blowing her nose.

There were enough bizarre happenings in this small town to make Charlotte certain there was more to this world than we could see and feel.

She would visit the one person she thought could give her some insight. The oldest woman in the village. Marielle was rumored to have the sight. Maybe she could tell Charlotte what had happened to Lucy and Melinda. She snorted. It wasn't like the cops had a clue.

Charlotte knocked on the bright blue door. Marielle opened it, beckoning her in. "I've been expecting you."

"Melinda is dead. At least, that's what the police officer told me. He said she was visiting Falconburg Castle and jumped to her death out of grief. I don't know why she went there but I do know this. She would not kill herself."

Charlotte wiped the tears from her eyes and blew her nose. She met the gypsy woman's wise eyes.

"Can you please tell me what happened to my sisters?"

The woman shuffled a worn deck of tarot cards. She laid them out in three rows of seven, from left to right.

"The top row is your past. The center row the present. And the bottom row is your future."

Marielle looked at the cards for a long time.

"You will find your sisters in England. But not this England."

"Melinda saw a painting in London. She swore it was of our sister Lucy. It was painted during the fourteenth century. Do you mean I can actually go back in time?"

"What is time? Time does not flow in a line. It is a circle. There are many possibilities if only you listen."

The woman gathered up the cards and put them away. She took Charlotte's hands in hers, looking at her palms.

"Be wary, child. Great danger awaits you. Look for the raven. He will guide your path. And the unicorn will bring great change to your life. Be ready."

Unicorns? Charlotte believed in a lot of things, things others called New Age or ridiculous. But even she didn't believe in unicorns.

"Thank you, Marielle. It's time for me to leave. To go home and prepare."

The little old gypsy lady kissed her on each cheek.

"Be strong, Charlotte. Your destiny awaits, if you have the courage to take it."

If Lucy had gone back in time, did the gypsy mean Melinda had found a way to go back too? Charlotte needed to research and prepare. She didn't know how she could go back, only that she must.

She grabbed her meager belongings and stuffed them into the back of the waiting taxi. While it made more sense to fly to England from Romania, she needed to go back to Holden Beach first. Tie up loose ends. Say goodbye to her childhood home and figure out a plan. Her sisters might call her flighty and free-spirited, but she had a knack for figuring things out.

She didn't have a will, and there was the house and cars to deal with. Charlotte pulled out a small notebook from her bag and started a list. The fact that Lucy never returned and now Melinda was missing told Charlotte once you ended up in the past, you were stuck. So she would take care of what she needed to and then catch a flight to England. And somehow she would find a way to travel through time and find her sisters. Though what if they ended up in different times?

"No!"

"Miss?"

"Sorry. I was talking to myself."

The driver nodded and went back to humming. Lucy and Melinda had to be together. Fate couldn't be so cruel.

Holden Beach, North Carolina

A month had passed since Charlotte returned home to Holden Beach. She was completely healed from the burns on her arms and legs from the fire. Thanks to an old recipe of Aunt Pittypat's, she wouldn't scar.

Charlotte noticed her finger shaking as she switched off the iPad. *Melinda Merriweather, American, apparent suicide due to grief over losing her sister, who died almost a year ago. Both sisters drowned and were presumed lost at sea.*

Two of her sisters go to England and are presumed dead or missing? Something smelled worse than a pot of collards left on the stove for two days and two nights.

Why hadn't she listened to Melinda? Gone with her? And what was with the Brits wanting to kill all three of them? She'd barely escaped the fire. Had come to believe someone was still after her. Why?

There had to be a reason. Charlotte jumped on her bike and rode to the local bookstore. Inside she perused the stacks. She bought books on the history of England, particularly those with a focus on the fourteenth century. Books on field medicine, plants, and herbs. Oh, and let's not forget books on witchcraft and New Age ideas. As she took the huge stack up to the checkout, the cute guy wearing glasses flirted with her.

"Wow, that's a lot of information. Are you studying for a class?"

"You could say that. I'm going to England for vacation, so I thought it would be fun to visit a few castles."

He picked up the book on field medicine. "Well, unless you're planning to start a war while you're there, I don't think you'll need this one."

"It's always good to broaden your horizons, don't you think?"

Charlotte collected her purchases and filled up the basket on the bike. One thing to check off her list. While she hated taking any more time before she left for England, she felt it was important to be prepared. Her flight left two weeks from today. That should give her enough time to read through the books and make notes. She was a firm believer in notes.

As Charlotte sat outside on the deck overlooking the ocean, she opened the leather-bound journal she'd purchased in the store. It was expensive compared to the cheapie notebooks she usually bought. But it looked old, so it shouldn't arouse suspicion if anyone saw it.

She planned to fill it with anything she might need during her journey. Moments in history, various plants used for healing, and, of course, Aunt Pittypat's famous recipes. All of them would go in the journal. Charlotte had a friend who might be able to get her antibiotics. That seemed like the one thing she wanted to take back with her.

A solar charger and phone so she could play music would be nice, but she decided against it. She didn't know why, but she was afraid to have too many modern things with her when she tried to go back in time.

Thanks to the power of the internet, she'd done most of her research online. There were a group of history buffs in Northern England she planned to meet up with. They'd been emailing back and forth. One of the guys said he'd teach her how to use a knife. He didn't think she would have long enough for him to teach her to use a sword. That was fine. One weapon would do.

No way could she take a knife on the plane. She'd buy an antique when she arrived. Flying into London would be perfect. Charlotte could scour some of the shops looking for the rest of what she needed. Things like a cloak and clothes to help her blend in. She could sew reasonably well, so she planned to add pockets to anything that didn't come with them.

As she ate a slice of pizza, Charlotte opened the first book and began reading.

Chapter Two

Charlotte leaned back in the rocking chair on the deck, staring at the water. She finished the glass of sweet tea with a soft sigh. "Guess I won't be getting any more of this where I'm going."

"Talking to ghosts?"

"Jake, you scared me. Want a drink?"

She grinned as he glanced at his watch. "I guess it's not too early for a beer. Based on your cryptic text, I have a feeling I'm going to need it."

She walked across the cool tiled floor to the blue and white kitchen. For a moment she hesitated before opening the cute retro turquoise refrigerator. Before long, if she were successful, refrigerators would no longer exist.

The door swung open and Charlotte let the blast of cold air soothe her nerves. She pulled out a beer for Jake, poured another glass of sweet tea for herself, and stood watching the condensation run down the cup. Maybe she should make a mojito? No, she needed to be fully functioning as she finalized the last few items on her list.

"I'm going to miss all this."

"I thought you were only going to England for a couple weeks. You know I'll be happy to housesit for as long as you need. Now that my apartment is turning condo, I've got to find a new place."

Charlotte put her bare feet up on the railing, admiring the sparkly purple polish. She reached into the tote bag next to the rocker and pulled out a file folder decorated with pink flamingos. She slid it across the table.

"What's this?"

"I'm going to be gone a lot longer than two weeks if everything works out as planned. If I don't come back, if they tell you I'm dead, the house is yours. Along with all the furnishings and my car. Though there won't be much money. I'm going to need most of it for my preparations."

She waved a hand around. "You'll be the sole owner of this incredible view. I never tire of looking at the ocean. The changing colors. How the sky meets water. Promise you'll take good care of the place."

Jake sputtered and coughed, choking on his beer. Charlotte helpfully pounded him on the back.

"You okay?"

He wiped his mouth with a napkin. "Are you out of your ever-loving mind? Time travel is only something that happens in the movies." He reached out across the small table, touching her arm.

Charlotte resisted the urge to laugh. The look on his face was so grave. Her smile faded as she realized his tone was one of someone speaking to a small child. She hated the condescending tone, heard it too many times during her life.

"Watch it, Jake. Keep up that tone and I'll leave the house to one of my favorite charities."

"You have to accept Lucy and Melinda are gone. I know you're sad. So am I. The thought of losing them and your aunt in one fell swoop would make anyone a bit batty."

Jake drank half of the beer. "You have to accept the facts. They are dead. And time travel isn't real. No matter what that crazy witch told you in Romania. Your sisters both dying while visiting some spooky old castle was terrible. But it's nothing more than coincidence. They did not travel through time."

He looked at her, his face full of pity. And in that instant, Charlotte wanted to smack the look off his face. She wasn't unhinged. Jake was her best friend, though sometimes she wished she could turn him into a fly and squash him.

"Do you want the house or not?"

"Listen, Charlotte," Jake pleaded, "don't go to England. In your frame of mind, you're susceptible to all kinds of suggestions. I really think you should see a doctor. They can give you some medication. Help you."

"Medication? That's the problem with this country. Too many people take medication for problems they don't have. If they would just get up, go outside, and take a walk, get some sun and do something silly once in a while, everyone would be in a better frame of mind. Not to mention cutting out all of that awful processed junk food that Big Food has us all addicted to. That alone would probably fix half the problems in this country."

Jake held up his hands. "Okay, okay, no need to get on your soapbox."

She was breathing through her mouth. Her skin felt clammy and hot at the same time. "I'm sorry. You touched a nerve." Charlotte rocked back and forth. "My mind is made up, and nothing you say will change it. This is something I have to do."

He slowly opened up the folder, looking at the papers inside. "I can't believe you're giving me the house. This place is amazing. You know I've always loved it."

Deep breaths, in and out. She listened to the waves crashing against the shore, the seagulls calling. After a few minutes, Charlotte was calm again. Centered. She placed her hand over his.

"I know how much you love the house. I'll feel better knowing the house is loved. I talked to the lawyer. Everything is in order. All that's left for me to do is to get rid of a few more things and finish my research."

She stood and paced along the deck. "Things aren't the same. I hear Aunt Pittypat's voice wherever I go. Lucy and Melinda...you can't imagine the hole in my heart." Charlotte searched his face, willing him to understand.

"Look at it this way: if I don't come back, you know I made it and you get the house. If I do come back, well, you've had a place to stay."

Jake scratched his chin. "I won't say anything more. I know you well enough by now to know when your mind is set. When do you leave?"

"The Friday of Memorial weekend. You get to enjoy the craziness all the crowds will bring."

"Won't matter to me. All I have to do is step out the back door and I'm on the beach."

She leaned against the rail, flicking the white paint off with a nail. Another item she could check off her list. There was nothing left for her here in North Carolina. It was time to go.

"I know you don't want to hear it, but I believe with all my heart and soul that somehow Lucy and Melinda traveled back in time. I'm going to find out what happened to them. Hopefully, find both of them."

Charlotte hugged Jake. "Go ahead and bring your stuff over. You already have a key." She gave him a little shove. "Don't worry—the beer in the fridge is yours. I never could stand the stuff."

He looked like he was about to start lecturing her again, but instead he pressed his lips together and kept quiet. He always had her back, even when he didn't agree with her. A true friend.

"I can never thank you enough for giving me a house on the beach. When you come back—" He held up a hand. "*If* you come back, I'll be here to pick up the pieces."

He kissed her on the forehead. "And if by some chance you don't come back, I'll know you made it." Jake stood back. "Try and find a way to send me a sign, okay?"

"Pinky swear." She held out her pinky and watched as he shook his head before pressing his pinky to hers. "Thanks, Jake. I'll miss you."

Charlotte watched him leave. As the screen door swung closed, she pulled up her favorite playlist, made a mojito, and went back outside to watch the sun set over the ocean.

North Carolina had been home her entire life. Sure, she'd traveled to lots of other countries, but knowing you always had a place to call home made all the difference. If she was right, then very soon she'd be calling medieval England home.

No more feeling sad or worrying. She blew a kiss to the sun as it fell into the ocean then went inside. Not at all tired, she decided stay up and finish sorting through the rest of the stuff in the house. There wasn't much left to go through. She'd already donated a lot of stuff, gave more to friends, and sorted through every drawer and closet.

The next day, Charlotte blew a strand of hair out of her face and wiped the grime from her cheek, letting the salty air coat her skin. Everything was done. She pulled out her trusty planner and went over the list again. The guys in England had promised to teach her how to use a knife.

She hoped the other information she'd learned during her research would be useful. Well, to a point. Heaven help anyone she might have to stitch up. Sewing a button on was one thing. Sewing skin together? Yuck.

She patted the leather journal. Knowledge was priceless.

Charlotte looked to the sky. "If you're listening, Aunt Pittypat, please don't let me end up in the wrong time."

The Black Plague took place smack in the middle of the century. Heaven forbid she ended up when that was going on. There still wasn't a cure even in this day and age. The small glass jar full of antibiotics made her feel a little bit better.

Had her sisters found someone to love in the past? Charlotte had searched and searched, but couldn't find the painting Melinda swore she saw in the museum in England. There was no listing for it on the website. She even called. A nice woman with the most perfect accent had assured her if they had it, she'd know. The hair on her arms had stood up as she ended the call. Had Melinda done something when she went back? Somehow changing history?

Honestly, Charlotte didn't care what her sisters had done to change history as long as she found them. It would be enough for her to see them again. For all of them to live in the same country, in the same time. To know they'd found love and were content.

And if she was very lucky, perhaps she would find her very own knight in shining armor.

The wind blew, it started to sprinkle, and for a moment Charlotte swore she heard the sound of bagpipes playing the most haunting melody. Weird.

Chapter Three

May 1330—England

"You ride slower than my grandmother," Sir Antoine called over his shoulder as he galloped through the wood.

Henry Thornton, Lord Ravenskirk, urged the horse faster. He'd spent the past fortnight at Sir Antoine's estate on his way back home from court. Hunting and drinking while Antoine invited all the daughters of eligible nobles so he could choose a wife.

Let them come. Henry had no desire to find a wife. His life was made up of fighting and drinking, which suited him perfectly. Let his elder brothers settle down. He would remain unwed.

Antoine veered left, and Henry laughed. Up ahead was a shortcut that would take him across the wood and bring him out in front of the stag. At some point Henry must have taken a wrong turn, for he found himself in an unfamiliar part of the wood.

What was that noise? Henry strained to listen. The sound was coming from the west. Quietly, Henry slid off the horse and tied the beast to a tree.

"Don't want you wandering off while I do my chivalrous duty."

The horse twitched an ear but remained silent. With a hand on the hilt of his sword, Henry made his way through the woods, following the sound of rushing water.

He came to a waterfall. At the base near an outcropping of rock, there was something in the water. He squinted and made out the color purple.

"Help me."

'Twas a woman's voice. Henry scrambled down the rocks, slipping and sliding. He landed on his backside with a thud.

"Bloody hell." He climbed across the moss-covered wet rocks and leaned over, reaching out.

"Give me your hand."

The woman looked up at him, her face wrinkled with age, yet there was great intelligence behind her eyes. And something much older. She reached out, lost her tenuous grip, and went under again.

The old woman surfaced. "My foot is stuck." She gasped and went under again, splashing and flailing.

Henry leaned forward as far as possible without falling in. He grasped her hand in his and felt the wet skin slip free. This time the water held her longer. He swore.

She surfaced, coughing. "I cannot break free. Leave me before the water claims you as well."

"Damnation. Do not give up." Henry removed his weapons, tunic, and boots. Bare-chested, he dove into the water, one knife in hand, and came up sputtering. "Bloody hell, that's cold."

With a few strokes he reached the woman, pulling her upward. She was shivering and her lips were blue. Henry dove under. The water was clear. He could see her foot trapped in the tree, her skirts caught on branches. Henry cut through the heavy fabric. Running out of breath, he surfaced, pulling her up again.

"Once more."

He went under again to free her foot. As he surfaced, Henry pulled her close. "Put your arms around my neck." With her on his back, he swam to shore. The bank was muddy as Henry pulled her out of the water.

"You are safe now." With a muttered curse, he lay there, looking up at the sky, panting. He had to quit eating so much and lazing about his hall. He was running to fat.

When he recovered his breath, Henry sat up. "How did you fall in?"

"Thank ye for saving me." The woman had long silver hair braided down her back. With a grace that belied her age, she rolled to her feet, the purple cloak sodden and dripping. Her dress and cloak were ragged around the edges.

He winced. "My apologies for your dress."

She looked down and wriggled her toes. "No matter. In my youth, I would have rewarded you with a kiss."

As he watched, she pulled off brush and unearthed a

basket and shoes. Something about her made Henry uneasy. He managed a weak smile.

"I was out foraging for herbs. I heard a voice and a man struck me. He believed me dead, tossed me into the water." Her hand went to her neck as if seeking something.

"Did you lose something, mistress?"

"My purse and my necklace. A verra powerful piece. The necklace is blessed and brings the wearer great fortune and luck."

"It doesn't seem to have brought you much luck on this day. Perchance it isn't working?"

The woman laughed, a tinkling sound like rain on armor filling the air. "Mayhap, young lord."

Henry looked around. "You are not far from the haunted wood. 'Tis known for a group of outlawed bandits. They live in the dark wood, venturing forth to prey on travelers and hold nobles and knights for ransom. 'Tis rumored they are led by a man who was once a rich and powerful knight. No one knows who he is."

She smiled. "I have nothing to fear from them."

Henry rolled his eyes. "Where's your guard?"

"I require no guard. The one who harmed me will pay." She eyed him as if waiting to see what he would say.

While he gathered up his clothing and re-sheathed his sword, Henry thought about what the woman said. A man who would ill use a woman so was no better than the lowest of men. He had a duty to see her where she needed to go.

He bowed. "Henry Thornton at your service. May I escort you to your destination, madam?"

"Aye, I knew by your handsome face and lovely hair I was rescued by one of the Thornton brothers. I think the most handsome of all the Thornton brothers, Lord Ravenskirk." The old woman beamed at him and took his arm.

Henry grinned as he lifted the woman up onto the horse. "You flatter me, madam. We should reach the inn by nightfall. My men will be waiting for me there."

They rode in companionable silence. As the sun sank low in the sky, she spoke.

"You will experience great upheaval in your life, Lord Ravenskirk."

"Please, call me Henry." He resisted the urge to snort. As one of five brothers, he was used to hearing all kinds of pronouncements. At a score and seven, Henry felt nothing could surprise him anymore. He had become inured to such tidings.

Oblivious to his musings, she went on. "Those you call friend will turn against you. A stranger will become more important to you than your own life. And when you see nothing but darkness ahead, look to the east."

Before he could retort, a raven called out overhead. And a feeling went through Henry, the feeling he sometimes got in battle or when something was about to happen. He would not jest. The old woman was more than she seemed. It was rumored a great healer, or some said witch, lived in the wood with the bandits. Could this be her? Not wanting to risk angering her, Henry kept his mouth shut.

The raven flew away as they rode out of the wood. He

kept the horse to the muddy path. In the distance he could see a small village. He would see her safely settled with a few coins. A feeling of foreboding coursed through him as Henry wondered what was coming next.

Chapter Four

Late May—England

Charlotte stretched, turning her head side to side to work out the kinks. While she was slightly taller than average at five foot seven, it wasn't *that* much of a difference. It seemed the seats on planes were shrinking. And the space between her knees and the seat in front of her? Nonexistent. Every time she flew, people were grumpy, the flights overbooked, and the air always smelled funny.

Her legs were achy from being scrunched up the entire flight. The man in front of her had reclined his seat all the way back and snored so loudly Charlotte found it impossible to sleep.

"That's what you get for flying coach. Why didn't you splurge for first class? Especially if this insane plan works and you'll never set foot on another airplane again."

Wow. That gave her pause. No more planes. The sound of cars, trains, and the hum of electrical wires. It would be so quiet in the past.

A businessman walking past her look alarmed as she talked to herself. He moved as far away from her as he could as he continued talking on his mobile phone. Charlotte stuck her tongue out at him. And no more people on their phones, ignoring everything around them.

She snorted. If he thought she was crazy, he should've met her famous great-grammy, Lucy Lou Merriweather. From the family stories she'd heard, her gram took crazy to a whole 'nother level.

A scruffy-looking guy, wearing jeans and a faded red t-shirt proclaiming *Bacon is Amazin,* held up a sign with her name on it.

"Maybe not to the pig." She smiled. "Hi, I'm Charlotte."

"Huh?" He looked down. "Right. The shirt. Funny." He cocked his head, a skeptical look plastered across his face. "You're the bird wants to learn how to use a knife and survive in medieval times?" He looked her up and down. "No offense, but you look more like a model than a chick who likes to play in the dirt."

"Looks can be deceiving. Shall we get going?"

The guy sighed. "Guess you got a mountain of luggage waiting?"

Charlotte nudged her rolling bag with her toe and showed him the messenger bag and backpack. "Nope. I travel light. Now, want to get going, or are we going to stand here and discuss hair-care products?"

The guy chuckled. "You're all right, Charlotte, the Yank from North Carolina." He waggled his eyebrows at her. "We could share a bottle tonight."

"Not gonna happen."

He simply shrugged and started walking. Thank goodness this wasn't the guy in charge. She'd end up smacking him before her two weeks were up. Why did some guys see an attractive woman and immediately assume she was stupid, helpless, and easy?

A beat-up truck covered in stickers was to be her chariot. He shot her a look, daring her to complain. Whatever. She'd ridden in a truck full of camels in the middle of summer. This was nothing. Charlotte stashed her bags behind the seat, climbed in, and twisted her hair up into a bun.

She must've fallen asleep. When she opened her eyes, the landscape had changed from the city to lush, verdant rolling hills. With a deep breath, Charlotte inhaled. The air tasted clean and full of growing things.

Covering her mouth as she yawned, she shifted in the seat. "Tell me about this camp in the woods."

"We're not allowed to stay in the castle ruins, so we set up a camp on the grounds. The castle must've been something back in the day. We've got permission to stay here for the summer. Pretty rustic. So if you're hoping for room service, you're out of luck."

Instead of telling the guy what he could do with his comment, Charlotte decided to keep quiet. She needed their knowledge. Who cared if he thought she was some beach Barbie playing in the dirt?

"I'll manage. Don't worry about me."

They drove for a while longer, and just as Charlotte was

ready to ask him to pull over so she could stretch her legs, the castle ruins came into view. Big houses weren't her thing. Give her a small cottage on the water and she'd be happy to grow old there.

There were tents set up and people dressed in medieval clothing. Some of the guys were practicing their sword skills, and others seemed to be working on various projects. There were a few women about, most in dresses, though she spotted two wearing shorts.

"Is that bread I smell?" Charlotte's stomach rumbled.

"Yep. We'll get you a bite then I'll show you to your tent."

"Sounds good to me."

As they walked through the camp, Charlotte nibbled the piece of bread, taking in every detail. They came to a tent set slightly away from the others. She was grateful it was already set up. No matter how many times she tried, it always took several attempts and lots of swearing before the tent wouldn't collapse on her head.

"This will be your home for the next two weeks. Once you get settled, come on over to where Mary is baking and I'll introduce you to Guy. He's in charge."

He left her without a glance. Charlotte looked around the inside of the tent. Nice. There was a cot with a pillow and blankets, a tiny dresser, and a comfy-looking chair.

She snorted. Her accommodations here were much nicer than some she'd lived in during her travels. There wasn't much to unpack. Did she dare leave her journal here in the tent? No, she'd keep it with her at all times. Charlotte slid it back in the messenger bag. This way she could take notes whenever she needed to. The bag wasn't waterproof, but she'd put the journal inside a plastic bag and sealed it.

The water in the pitcher on the dresser was cold. She poured a bit in the basin and splashed some on her face. Her bun had come undone and it was windy, so Charlotte braided her long blonde hair so it wouldn't blow in her face. As she was looking for an elastic to secure the end, something bright fluttered under the cot. She leaned down and pulled a scrap of blue ribbon out. It looked new, almost as if someone had placed it there. She tied it around the braid and made her way out of the tent. People looked her over with open curiosity as she walked through the camp. She smiled but kept going. Plenty of time to get to know everyone later.

"You must be the American?"

"Charlotte. You must be Mary. I had a small taste of your bread. The smell is making me drool."

The woman standing in front of her was plump, with short, spiky brown hair, and a huge smile on her face. A tattoo of a dragon circled her neck and looked like it went down her shoulder.

She handed Charlotte a slice of bread. "There's honey in the bread. That's the secret."

Mary looked to be in her late thirties to early forties, if Charlotte had to guess. She was pretty good with ages. She was wondering why the woman was here, when Mary spoke as if she'd heard what Charlotte was thinking.

"My son got married and moved to Australia. My husband died five years ago. I decided I couldn't knit another pair of socks without stabbing someone with my knitting needles, so I looked around for something else to do. I went on a dig in Egypt and decided it was fun. Through someone there I found this group. We travel around to different locations around the UK. It's been interesting."

She handed Charlotte another piece of bread, thickly spread with butter. "So what brings you here? We don't get many Yanks."

"I too found myself with time on my hands and a yearning to do something different." Charlotte crossed her fingers behind her back. She wasn't ready to tell this group of people why she was here. Not to mention they might think she was completely out of her mind.

"You know how things are in America. The crime and all. I thought it would be a good idea to learn how to use a knife and see what it was like to live so long ago." She took a big bite of the bread. "This reminds me of the bread my favorite aunt used to make. I think I could eat the whole loaf."

Mary laughed. "Come along, luv. I'll introduce you to Guy, the man in charge."

There were several men fighting in pairs with swords. Mary led her over to a group of metal chairs. They sat down and watched. Charlotte had to admit, they looked pretty good. One man in particular seemed completely serious about what he was doing. As she watched them, doubt filled her. Could she do this? Was she really going to try to go back in time?

Charlotte shook her head. There was no more time for doubts. No more time to question herself. Positive thoughts only from here on out. You had to tell the universe what you wanted and believe it would deliver.

The guy she thought was the best at fighting bowed to his opponent and slid his sword into an ornate scabbard at his waist.

"Charlotte, right?" He wore what looked like a pair of dark green leggings. The image of the Jolly Green Giant popped into her head, and she had to bite the inside of her cheek to keep from busting out laughing. The jingle from the commercial kept running through her brain.

Mary seemed to know what Charlotte was thinking, for she elbowed her in the side and gave her a look.

"Nice to meet you. Thanks again for having me."

"Like I said when we chatted online, I'm not sure how much I can teach you in two weeks. Can you stay longer?"

"No, I'm afraid I only have two weeks. So whatever we can cram into the time would be great. I'm not afraid of hard work and I don't need a lot of sleep."

The breeze tickled the back of her neck, cooling her as the sun shone down. She tilted her head, listening. Yes, it was the sound of someone playing pipes. Almost the same music she thought she'd heard before she left home.

Charlotte opened her mouth to say something, but noticed the look on the others' faces. Guy and Mary were looking at each other, and some of the others had stopped what they were doing and were looking around, looks of astonishment on their faces.

"What? You hear the piper too?"

Guy stared at her. "This castle belonged to Edward

Thornton. The oldest of five brothers. As the story goes, one of the Thornton ladies saved the men from certain death." He narrowed his eyes at her. "This is the first time we've heard him."

"You know, it's funny, I thought I heard the same melody playing right before I left North Carolina."

Mary sucked in a sharp breath and looked at Guy. He looked just as interested.

"What am I missing?" They were looking at Charlotte like she had two heads.

"The legend says the piper haunts the Thornton castles. He only plays for the lady of the castle. I thought you said your last name was Merriweather?"

"It is."

"Is that your married name? Was someone in your family named Thornton?"

Jeez, this guy was intense. "I've never been married. And no one in my family was named Thornton."

Charlotte tilted her head up and closed her eyes, letting the music wash over her. "It sounds so sad and lonely yet calming at the same time."

"There's more to you than meets the eye, Charlotte Merriweather," Guy said. The piper finished his tune and it was silent. After a few minutes, the spell broke and everyone went back to what they were doing.

"You're sure you're not just playing that for my benefit out of some hidden speakers? You really expect me to believe there's a ghost haunting the castles?"

He shrugged. "We weren't playing any music. No one

uses their phone or tablet until they turn in for the night. Technology is banned during the day. We've never heard the famed piper play before. As I said, it's only a legend, but he must think you're a Thornton, otherwise he wouldn't play for you."

Chapter Five

Charlotte rubbed her wrists. There were bruises running up and down her arms in varying shades of black and blue, to older greens and yellows. More than she'd had over her entire childhood combined. Spending the days learning so much new stuff was exhausting. She hadn't gone to college; instead she went on a dig her last year of high school and was hooked on the travel bug. Hitting the books made her head ache.

Learning how to use a knife and stitch a wound, basic plant medicine, customs, and history. All of it was enough to make her long for a beach, a good book, and a nap. Even her hair was tired.

Though the good thing about being so busy was how time passed in a blur. The days blending together into one long day. They were located in Northern England, and all she'd seen so far was the camp and the tiny village. Not exactly much time for sightseeing. Only one brief visit to restock a few essentials.

The people in the village treated them as if they were all a bit off their rockers, but they smiled and were nice enough. It was funny; no matter where you went, people commented on her accent. No one ever thought they had an accent. She could get used to the lovely British accents she'd heard over the past couple of weeks.

The smack across the back of her knuckles jerked Charlotte out of her thoughts. "Ouch!"

"Pay attention. I could've killed you three times by now."

Charlotte bent her knees and thrust out with her left hand. Charlie, the guy who'd picked her up when she flew into London, jumped back.

"Much better. Again."

She thrust upward with the wooden knife. Yesterday they'd made her practice with a real knife on a side of beef. The first couple of times the knife went into the meat, Charlotte's stomach dropped. She'd thrown up in the bushes. They'd teased her ever since.

"Come on, Barf Barbie, you can do better than that. You don't want to vomit when you're trying to stab one of the bad guys, do you? What, do you think he'll be so disgusted by the stench he'll go away? Not likely, luv."

At least it was a compliment she was now practicing with Charlie and Guy. Everyone in camp said they were the two best fighters. She sent up thanks to Aunt Pittypat for all those dance lessons when she was young. They'd obviously helped with her balance.

Charlotte found she was somehow able to anticipate what her opponent was going to do before he did it. While

LONELY IS THE KNIGHT

she wasn't sure she'd actually be able to kill anyone, she'd started to feel comfortable enough that she wouldn't cut off her own finger.

Looking like she knew what she was doing should deter the lazy bad guys. And if she drew blood, maybe the rest would leave her alone.

Charlie came at her. Charlotte leaned back into a partial backbend—thank you, yoga—then straightened, stepped in, and grinned as she noted the surprise on his face. Her wooden blade pressed against his neck.

"Who's the Barbie now?"

Charlotte stepped back, the knife gripped in her left hand. They were both breathing heavily, though she was the only one doubled over and panting. He looked angry, like someone stole his last cookie. It was the first time she'd gotten the better of him, and it felt good. Really freaking good.

Charlotte noticed he tended to get cocky as he fought, and leaned to the right when he thrust. Some of the people watching started to laugh.

"Well done," Guy said. "When you first showed up, as pretty as you are, we all thought you'd go home after the first day or two. But you stuck it out. I'm right proud of you. Sure you don't want to stay a while longer and learn how to use a sword?"

Charlotte lifted the braid off the back of her neck, letting the breeze cool her off. She was dressed in a pair of leggings and a t-shirt proclaiming *Cats rule, dogs drool*. Sweat tickled as it dripped down her ribcage.

"I wish I could, but I think a sword is way too heavy for me. I'll stick with the knife." She handed the wooden blade back to him.

"Don't forget the shop I told you about."

Over dinner last night, Guy had told her where to go to buy a shiny new knife. Charlotte didn't want new. She wanted antique, something that would blend in.

"I'll remember. I can't thank you all enough."

While she had enjoyed her time with the group of history buffs, the feeling it was time to go had been growing stronger over the past few days. Tomorrow was the day. She didn't know why, only that she needed to get back to London tomorrow. It felt like time was running out.

An almost hot shower left her feeling refreshed and not quite as sore. One of the guys had rigged up a couple of solar showers. It was a much-appreciated luxury. Back at her tent, Charlotte threw on a pair of yoga pants and a t-shirt, grabbed her journal, and sat down in a chair outside the tent. The east side faced an open meadow, with a low stone wall in the distance. She could almost see knights charging across the field, their colors bright against the sun.

"Bet you could use this." Mary handed her a mug of wine.

Charlotte sniffed. "Apricot?" She took a small sip, the fruity wine sliding down her throat. "Now that's refreshing. I like it better than the dandelion batch you made last week."

"The dandelion recipe needs a bit of work. It's missing something."

"It tasted kind of like whisky."

"I'm going to make up another batch of apricot next week." The chair creaked as Mary leaned back and closed her eyes. Charlotte had grown fond of the older woman during her time here.

Mary was forty-two, though she looked a good ten years younger. It was hard to believe she was twenty years older than Charlotte, old enough to be her mom. The twinge in her heart made her take a few deep breaths. She would miss her new friend.

"You're always scribbling away in that journal. Are you writing a book?"

Charlotte ran her hand across the leather cover. "No, just useful tidbits. I like to make lists and write things down. Never know when the knowledge might come in handy."

"Speaking of handy, thanks for the face cream recipe. It's amazing. Think I'll try a batch with roses next time."

Aunt Pittypat would be over the moon to know others were finding her recipes useful. Charlotte was grateful for her time here. She'd learned so much. Given the time she had set aside, she was as prepared as she could possibly be. Too bad there wasn't a guidebook for time traveling.

"I'll miss you. You've been so kind to me."

Mary leaned over to pat her shoulder. "Take care of yourself, luv. I won't ask the real reason you're here. I respect your need for privacy. Hearing the piper play every afternoon for you makes me sure there's something else going on. Perhaps some task you are meant to complete."

"Maybe he'll keep playing after I'm gone."

Mary shook her head. "No. My bet is you'll hear him in

London."

Instead of saying anything, Charlotte took another sip of the wine. "I admire you for embarking on a new adventure. So many people get set in their ways. You inspire me."

Mary looked embarrassed. "I'll see you off in the morning."

Alone with her thoughts, Charlotte stared off into the distance. A while later she opened the journal, paging through the entries for the umpteenth time. When she returned to London tomorrow, she planned to visit the museum.

While the woman had told her there was no painting, she wanted to see for herself. In case there was another painting that caught her eye. She knew the odds of seeing either of her sisters in a painting hanging on the walls of a museum was like winning the lottery, but she had to try. Then after a lunch of fish and chips, she'd hit the antique shops.

A woman in the village had made her two dresses and a cloak while she'd been learning how to fight. Each garment had pockets, as requested, and a Velcro strip around the waist and hem, concealing a shallow, long pocket where she could hide the antique coins she hoped to purchase. They were nothing fancy, but Charlotte thought they would keep her from standing out.

Later that night after dinner, she packed up her meager belongings. She'd given a few things to some of the people here. Stuff she would no longer have any use for.

The next morning, after a quick breakfast, Charlotte looked around. Would this place look very different in the past? Would the castle be standing with people going about their everyday lives?

As she shut the door of the truck, the haunting melody started to play. A few days ago she thought she'd caught a glimpse of the ghostly piper. He was on top of one of the crumbling towers. She made out blue clothes and brown hair. She'd waved, but he hadn't acknowledged her.

Charlie rolled his eyes. "While I don't mind the pipes once in a while, enough is enough."

"You're just jealous."

"Might be." As he drove away, the sounds faded. Did the piper truly play for her and her alone? And if he did, what did it mean?

What was the message?

Chapter Six

The healer insisted Henry leave her at a house in the village.

"I will visit with another healer and see you again."

He helped her off the horse. "As you wish." If he believed in otherworldly things, which he most certainly did not, Henry would have been awestruck by her power. Instead he was simply being chivalrous.

He threw the reins of his horse to a waiting boy. "Take good care of him." Henry flipped the boy a coin.

The child bit the coin and grinned. "Thank ye, my lord."

He entered the inn. It was hot and smelly.

"Henry, over here." Antoine leaned back against the wall with a wench on either side of him. He was playing cards with three other men.

He knew Antoine from the times he'd visited court. Sir Antoine would never think of others first. But as Antoine's home was on the way to Ravenskirk, Henry had been obliged to stop there.

Another wench brought him ale. "My lord. Is there

anything else you require?" She leaned down to display her considerable wares. While Henry loved the company of women, he left wenches to his knights.

"Care to lose a bit of your gold, Lord Ravenskirk?"

While Henry enjoyed competing in tourneys, he did not care overmuch for cards. Counting all those numbers made his head ache.

"Not tonight. I needs see to the men and horses."

He made his way out of the smoke-filled inn, to the stables. "Have you eaten, Adam?"

The boy had come to him by way of his brother Edward. He would serve as squire to Henry.

"Yes, my lord. I saw to the horses first."

"Sleep out here tonight. I don't like the looks of the men inside."

The boy nodded. Restless, Henry stroked the neck of his favorite horse. A few of his men found their way into the inn to drink and wench.

It was growing dark as Henry made his way back inside. Antoine and the men he was playing cards with were deep in their cups.

"One hand, Henry. Come, it seems I am short of gold."

Henry grimaced, but sat down to play one hand. Antoine threw the last of his coins onto the table, along with something else that glinted in the light.

"Where did you come by the trinket?"

He shrugged. "Payment for helping the healer. She was in here moments ago."

Henry was aghast. "'Tis not chivalrous."

"I care not." Antoine drank the rest of his ale; a bit dribbled out of the corner of his mouth, down his chin, and onto his tunic. "The witch cursed me."

"Do not jest." Henry felt a chill go through the room. He looked around for enemies, catching the eye of his men. He saw them stiffen. He shook his head. He didn't know what made him so nervous, only that he was. "In the woods earlier, did you throw her in the water?"

"Nay." Though Antoine looked guilty. "She said I would pay for stealing from her. I should have her beaten."

Henry spoke softly. "'Tis our duty to help those weaker than we. The healer is under my protection. You should not have demanded payment from her."

Henry picked up the necklace. He didn't know why, but something about it made him want to touch it. It was made of gold. With an emerald, a diamond, a sapphire, and a gold charm in the shape of a horse with a horn? No, 'twas a unicorn.

Antoine snatched it from his hand. "I need that to wager with, my friend."

Henry took Antoine's wrist and squeezed, making him gasp. "Let go."

The arrogant idiot let go of the necklace. Henry took it as the others started to protest. He dropped a bag on the table, the heavy clink quelling their outrage. He opened it and withdrew several pieces of gold, much more than the necklace was worth.

"This will suffice."

Everyone nodded. Satisfied, Henry tucked the necklace

into the pouch at his waist. He could stand it no more—he strode out of the inn. He needed to walk. To clear his head before he started a fight. His brothers were always lecturing him on thinking first before acting.

As he paced around the building, one of his men ran out, shouting, "Lord Ravenskirk, come quickly."

Henry sprinted inside. Antoine's face turned from crimson to purple. Everyone watched, looks or horror upon their faces. The healer stood in front of the table, her long silver hair unbound, the purple cloak wrapped tightly around her.

He pounded Antoine on the back. It was too late—the man fell headfirst into his plate.

One of the men playing cards said, "He choked on a bone."

Henry looked to the healer. She inclined her head to him and quietly made her way out of the inn. No one stopped her, though many crossed themselves as she passed. Had she truly cursed Antoine to die? No. Henry would not believe in curses. Antoine was a glutton. Anyone could choke on a bone and die.

The next morning, Henry and the men set out from the inn in a somber mood, most of the men still feeling the effects of the ale from the night before. After riding a few hours, they stopped alongside a stream.

Henry threw the reins to his squire. "I'm going to wash."

He hadn't had time that morning. Wanted nothing more than to be on his way home. He felt the urge to hurry. As he cupped water in his hands to drink, he heard a noise. Henry looked up to see the healer. She had a basket over her arm filled with green things.

He bowed. "Madam. My apologies."

She cocked her head at him. "For what, Lord Ravenskirk?"

He opened the pouch at his waist and withdrew the necklace. "In the commotion last night, I failed to return this to you. I did not know Antoine demanded your necklace in payment for helping you. There was no payment required."

He reached toward her to give her the necklace and found he could not let go. The piece clenched tightly in his fist. For a moment he hesitated. The healer watched him, a smile on her face, and shook her head.

"You will have need of it. Keep it close. For there is one who must have the necklace."

She leaned down to pick watercress growing at the edge of the stream. "The necklace will find its way back to me on its own when it is no longer needed."

Filled with relief, Henry tucked the necklace back into the pouch. He withdrew a handful of coins. "Take them." She shook her head, and he said, "Please, madam. I am sure you know those who have need of my gold."

She looked at him. Then she accepted the coins.

"May I escort you to wherever you're going?"

"I am quite safe in the wood. And you must go home. Do not tarry."

He wanted to ask her why, but there was something otherworldly going on, and Henry decided against it.

"You will make a good husband." And with that remark, a shudder of fear ran through him. He had vowed never to marry. Never have a woman scolding him day and night. Filled with hatred whenever she looked upon his face. Henry turned and made his way back to the men.

Chapter Seven

"You enjoy now, miss."

"Smells delicious." Charlotte left the chip shop and made her way to a park across the street, where she found a bench and sat down to eat lunch. It was fun to people-watch. To make up stories of what they did for a living, who they loved, and their favorite place to travel.

The visit to the museum had ended up being a bust. No painting with anyone resembling Lucy. Nothing at all about either of her sisters. Realistically, she hadn't expected to find anything. But she had to wonder. Melinda had been sure she'd seen the painting of Lucy. So what had happened to it? The only explanation Charlotte could come up with was that Melinda or Lucy had done something to change time, and now the painting no longer existed today.

Why hadn't she gone with Melinda when she called? If she had, maybe they'd all be together. Then again, Charlotte was assuming her sisters ended up in the same time and place. How awful it would be to go back in time and be in the wrong year or country.

Her heart beat faster, sweat dripped down her back, and everything around her sounded muffled. Something was wrong. Was she suddenly allergic to the fish? She couldn't breathe. Was she dying?

Time passed, and slowly her breathing returned to normal. The panic attacks had started when she was eighteen. Now she never knew what would trigger one.

Arriving back in London, spending time with the history buffs, and finalizing her affairs had made what she was about to attempt seem real. Charlotte noticed everything. The smell of exhaust from automobiles, the sounds of cars and trucks, the motion when riding the tube. People fascinated her. Seeing them hurrying to and fro, heads down and tapping away on their phones, even in restaurants.

She saw a family of four in a café. Mom, dad, and two kids. Everyone was on their phone, and there was silence at the table as they all typed away, oblivious to each other.

Then there was the overwhelming amount of choices. From the grocery store, to the bakery, and cheese shop. They could walk into the store and buy fruit and vegetables all year round, out of season.

Heck, most of the people she knew didn't even have to worry about where their next meal would come from. It didn't matter if it was winter; you simply went to the store. While rationally Charlotte knew things were going to be very different in the past, she was having a hard time wrapping her head around it.

She stood, threw the wrapper in the trash, and started

wandering. There were a bunch of shops on the other side of the park and, according to her guidebook, several antique shops. She turned the corner and tripped over an uneven cobblestone as she heard the music. That haunting melody.

"I know that song." Icy fingers stroked the back of her neck. Up ahead at the corner, she saw a man wearing a blue tunic and hose. He was playing the pipes. The man nodded to her, beckoning her forward. No one else seemed to notice him.

"I'm glad we had a family full of eccentric women or I might think I was hallucinating," she mumbled, rubbing her eyes. As she reached the corner, the piper vanished. Where to start? Charlotte slowly turned in a circle. There was a dusty-looking shop on one corner and a coin shop across the street. Perfect—she'd start with the money.

"Afternoon. Help ye, miss?"

Charlotte looked at the cases. There were so many different types of coins. How would she ever decide?

"I hope so." She crossed her fingers behind her back. "My grandfather loves old coins. And since it's his ninetieth birthday, I wanted to do something extra special. I'm interested in purchasing coins from medieval England, specifically from the early to mid-1300s."

The man wrinkled his brow, then his face brightened. "Have just the thing, I do. Back in a jiffy."

The man stepped behind the curtain, and Charlotte could hear cabinets opening and closing, the sound of boxes sliding around, and the tinkling of coins. The man pushed through the curtain, dust on his dark brown vest, his gray hair sticking out on the sides. "These will do quite nicely, I think." He set down a battered black leather case in front of her, opened it, and pulled out five trays.

"I must admit, I don't know a lot about coins, so I'll need to rely on your expertise."

"Did you have an amount in mind to spend?"

Charlotte opened her messenger bag and rifled through the contents. She came out with a small bag, which she opened, and placed a wad of cash on the counter.

"Ten thousand pounds." She knew it was a lot, but she wanted to be prepared. Who knew what she might run into? And it wasn't like she had kids or anyone to leave the money to. Jake was getting the house and the contents of her checking account, so the rest was hers to use. Oh, how Aunt Pittypat would have loved this adventure. She'd already bought eight thousand in gemstones. They were hidden in the lining of her messenger bag.

The man's brows went up, one of them twitching as if it were a caterpillar crawling across his face. He rubbed his hands together and grinned.

"Your grandfather is a lucky man to have such a generous granddaughter. We can do quite well with that amount."

The coin dealer sorted through the coins, setting some aside, mumbling to himself. Charlotte had a feeling it was going to take a while, so she wandered around the shop, stopping to look at whatever caught her eye. It was obvious the man loved what he did, had a love of history.

"Have you been doing this long? Collecting and selling

coins?"

The man looked up. "When I was a wee boy I found an old coin at the beach in Cornwall. Turned out it was from Roman times. Quite valuable. I was hooked." He scratched the tuft of hair behind his ear. "Had this shop nigh on forty years."

"It must be nice to be able to do what you love."

"After the missus died, it's what's kept me going." The man looked at the clock. "Care for a cup of tea?"

"I'd love one, thanks."

The man went in the back and came back with a tray and a kettle that had pictures of cows and pigs dancing arm in arm. There were two teacups and a package of biscuits. As he poured the tea, he told her about his childhood. Charlotte told him about losing her parents in a sailing accident when she was little. How her eccentric aunt raised she and her sisters. It felt good to talk about them. Somehow it kept them alive.

Though she left out the fact her sisters were gone and she was planning to attempt the impossible. Charlotte wiped her mouth with a cloth napkin. "Thank you, that was just what I needed. Shopping makes me hungry."

He chuckled. "And, I suspect, quite a bit poorer after this. Come see what I've picked out. It's a lovely selection. Your grandfather will be delighted."

They talked about the coins for a while, the man telling her the value of each and the year they were made. He was very knowledgeable. Charlotte was glad the ghostly piper had led her to him. As he wrote up the bill of sale, he blinked at her. "You're going to walk around carrying ten thousand pounds worth of antique coins?" He handed her a cloth bag that clunked when it landed on the counter.

"Look at me—I look like a hippie. No one's going to think I have anything worth stealing." She spun around in a circle. She was wearing a pair of black leggings so faded they looked gray, a short-sleeve long t-shirt with a picture of her favorite character from *The Walking Dead* on the front, and her battered messenger bag.

"You have a point."

She handed him the money, then put the cloth bag inside the messenger bag. As she started to leave, Charlotte turned around.

"Would you happen to know where I can find a leather worker or shoemaker?"

He looked at her, thinking. Maybe she should clarify. "I want to have a piece of leather stitched into my boot—you know, so I can hide something."

The man's face brightened. "Aye. It would be wise. Across the street and three shops down, you'll find what you need."

Charlotte thanked him and left the shop, the bell tinkling as the door closed behind her.

A little bit later, she came out of the leather shop. She was wearing a new pair of boots. The man had kept her old boots to work on while she shopped. The new boots already had the loops she wanted. Apparently it wasn't a crazy request. She told the man she would be performing as a wench in Renaissance festivals for the rest of the summer.

And wondered if he could add something to the boot so she could slide a knife in each—you know, to look authentic.

The man smiled and told her he had made several. He said to leave the boots and come back in a couple of hours. The beautiful brown leather boots in the window called to her, and she bought them. They fit like a glove, and while they were expensive, she thought it would be wise to have two pairs of shoes.

Charlotte heard the faint sound of pipes on the wind and found herself again in front of the dusty-looking shop. The sign was so faded all she could make out was the word *antiques*. It wasn't in her guidebook, and the window was so dusty and grimy it was hard to tell what was inside. Curious, she pushed open the door and went in, coughing from the dust the breeze stirred up.

Chapter Eight

The shop seemed to be a hodgepodge of antiques from various time periods. Charlotte poked through the shop waiting for the proprietor to appear. As she was looking through a cabinet, something purple sparkled. Given all the dust, Charlotte was surprised she noticed it at all. It was an amethyst bracelet set in gold. Leaves and flowers were carved into the gold. It was a beautiful piece with no price tag. She went up to the counter.

"Hello? Is anyone here?"

She heard a noise in the back, and a tiny, stooped woman with gray hair tottered through the door.

"Sorry, dearie, didn't hear you come in. Something catch your eye?"

Charlotte held out the bracelet. "I love this piece, but I didn't see a price tag. And I'm also looking for a couple of daggers. Something a woman might have used in medieval times. I'm going to be working at Renaissance fairs for the rest of the summer, and I want to look authentic." She was getting pretty good at all this fibbing.

The woman picked up the bracelet, turning it back and forth. "I remember this piece. It came in with a couple of blades." She tapped her forehead. "Now where did I put them?"

The woman thought for a moment then her face brightened. "I remember. That idiot Fred, he bought a box unseen. Thought he was getting a deal. But they got one over on him. The blades he swore were antique were only reproductions, and not very good ones. I sacked him." She muttered to herself and went into the back of the shop. Charlotte found her fascinating. A few minutes later, the woman came back and plunked two daggers on the counter.

"They're beautiful." Charlotte picked them up one at a time, admiring the handiwork. It was silly, but she felt the weight of history in her hands. Felt a connection to the daggers. Like they were meant for her.

The woman snorted. "Pretty enough. But not antique." She held up one of the blades, turning it back and forth, and Charlotte could see an inscription on the blade.

"See this? There are inscriptions on both blades. Must've been someone's idea of a joke."

"Why?"

The woman handed her the dagger. She'd learned enough to know how right the blade felt in her hand. The balance was good. Charlotte turned it back and forth, trying to read the inscription.

"I can't make out the wording."

"It's Norman French, but the saying is wrong for a

dagger." The shopkeeper held up the first blade. The one with the big amethyst in the hilt.

"See this one? It reads, *Om* over and over, and then *The sound of the universe smiling.*" The woman picked up the other blade, this one with a sapphire in the hilt.

"And this one says, *The soul is here for its own joy.*" She laid the blade down on the counter, a disgusted look on her face. "Utter rubbish. Some fool's idea of a joke."

Charlotte couldn't get enough air. She heard the shopkeeper's voice from far away, as if she were standing at the end of a long tunnel.

Not now. Please not now. She willed her mind to calm. Took slow, even breaths. She was shaky. Weak.

For she knew both of those sayings well. Intimately. Both of them were tattooed down her ribcage. It had to be a sign. Somehow she had gone back in time...or would go back in time? While she pondered the idea, the sound of what was becoming her favorite melody drifted through the shop.

"Never heard that tune before." The old woman squinted out the grimy windows. "Seen that boy earlier today, playing on the corner."

Since she didn't know what do say, Charlotte decided not to say anything. How could she when she couldn't explain what was happening?

Melinda, if you're listening, I'm so sorry for not believing you. For not coming with you. But I'm here now and I'm coming. Lead me to the right place and time.

The woman seemed to think her hesitation meant Charlotte was looking for a deal. She scowled at her. "I'll let you have both daggers and the bracelet for two hundred pounds."

The room stopped spinning, and Charlotte looked up at her, hands braced on the counter. "Since these are reproductions, they're really not worth much. And I only need props, nothing fancy. The bracelet is pretty, but how about one hundred and fifty? Cash?"

The woman nodded. "Done."

Charlotte noticed her hand shaking as she handed the money over. The woman started to wrap up the daggers, but Charlotte shook her head. "Let me see if they fit."

She leaned down and slid the dagger into the leather sheath inside the boot. It fit perfectly. While it felt a little bit strange, in time she would get used to it. The other one slid in the leather sheath. The boots were loose enough that the blades weren't uncomfortable. Charlotte took a deep breath, waiting. Nothing happened. Maybe she needed the bracelet too?

"Would you help me with the clasp?"

It sounded like the woman muttered *crazy Americans* as she fastened the bracelet around Charlotte's wrist.

"Thank you." Charlotte stood still. Nothing happened. She was sure the piper had led her to the shop, positive the inscriptions on the blades were meant for her. That somehow she must've been given them in the past.

So why weren't they working? Why hadn't she been transported back to medieval England?

"Are you sick, dearie?" The woman came around the counter and took her arm. She led Charlotte to a chair and pushed her down. A puff of dust rose as she sat.

"Stay here. I'll get you a glass of water." As the woman went to the back Charlotte, heard her say, "These women today, never eating enough. Too skinny."

Despair flooded every fiber of her being. Why was she still in modern England? Charlotte put her head between her knees, taking long breaths, willing her mind to quiet. Remembering her meditation.

A glass was thrust into her hand. "Drink some water, you'll feel better."

Charlotte took the glass of cold water and drank half of it. She was clammy and sweaty. She handed the glass back to the woman. "You've been very kind, thank you. I guess I need to go grab a bite to eat." She stood, swayed for a moment, and then found her center.

Back across the street, she paid for the work on her old boots and made her way back to the hotel in a daze.

Had she failed before she'd even begun?

Chapter Nine

Charlotte boarded the train for Falconburg Castle, her heart heavy. Why hadn't the daggers worked? There was no way the inscriptions would both exactly match her tattoos unless they were meant for her.

It was a three-hour ride to her destination. Maybe going back in time had something to do with one of the castles? There must be magic there. She brightened. Now that she had the daggers and bracelet, surely once she stood upon the spot where Melinda or Lucy vanished, she too would go back in time.

She planned to start at Falconburg, where Melinda disappeared. If the worst happened and she didn't go back, she would make her way to Blackford Castle, where Lucy vanished. One of the castles had to work.

Somehow she managed to fall asleep. The absence of motion woke her. Charlotte sat up to see people getting off the train. The voice on a speaker announced her stop. Gathering the backpack and messenger bag, she stepped off the train at Blackpool Station. It wasn't far, so she walked from the train station to the hotel.

There was Blackpool Tower in the distance. She'd read it was inspired by the Eiffel Tower. If she had time, she'd go check it out. Her room was cute and overlooked the promenade. Her stomach growled, reminding her she hadn't eaten since breakfast that morning at the hotel.

Fried fish probably didn't exist in the past, so Charlotte decided to get fish and chips again. She bought them from a man with a cheery green and white cart and walked along the promenade, people-watching. It felt good to stretch her legs after being on the train. Seeing the Irish Sea made her long for the Atlantic Ocean back home.

With the breeze off the water, Charlotte was glad she hadn't worn shorts. What did people do before leggings had been invented? As she was throwing the trash away, she noticed a guy watching her. What was it? Something about him seemed off. It was his body language.

Everyone else around was relaxed. Walking, doing their own thing, enjoying the warm day. This guy, though, he wore a jacket in the summer. And while he had on sunglasses, she could tell he was alert, completely focused on her, ignoring everything else around him.

She meandered down the promenade and suddenly knelt down to tie her espadrille. In the reflection from the shop to her right, she could see him following. He was keeping back far enough so she wouldn't notice, but he must not realize how out of place he looked. Who was he?

As she walked faster, Charlotte kept glancing around her.

She didn't see anyone else following her, just this guy. A car horn beeped, startling her.

"My brother is dead because of your sister." He jerked her by the elbow. Charlotte opened her mouth to scream then shut it with a snap as something sharp poked her in the side. After her time with the guys up north, she knew the feel of a knife.

"Scream and I'll gut you like a fish. My brother and I work for the same company. Told them I'd be happy to finish the job."

"Wait. Your brother was the jerk who tried to kill my sister? Simon died a long time ago. Why can't you people just let it go?"

He sneered at her. "It's the principle, luv."

Charlotte watched as a couple pulled up in a roadster. She tripped, jerking away from him. "I can't walk as fast as you. Hold on."

Without waiting for an answer, she leaned down and untied her shoes. She tied the long laces together and dangled them from her free hand. When she stood up, she turned around slowly, like she had all the time in the world. Completely unconcerned he could kill her.

"I love to go barefoot in the summer, don't you?" She looked down at her bright blue toes. All the while keeping an eye on the couple. The man spoke Italian. The woman with him was gorgeous, with long black hair, bright red lips, and legs for miles. She wore enough gold jewelry to tempt a pirate. The man put his hand on the woman's lower back, giving her bottom a little smack as they went inside a jewelry store.

Charlotte adored cars. Who in their right mind left an Aston Martin V12 Vantage S Roadster just sitting there, running? What kind of person did that?

Crazy pants, that's who. The car was a beautiful machine, except for the color. It was banana yellow. She cringed, feeling sorry for the Aston Martin. Driving that car, people would see it coming from miles away. But then again, that was probably the point, wasn't it?

Before she could overthink it, Charlotte stomped on her captor's foot as hard as she could. As he yelped, she twisted away from him, pressing down hard on the fleshy part of skin between his thumb and first finger, hitting a nerve. He yelled out and dropped the knife.

She made a run for it. Charlotte hopped in the car, threw it into gear, and took off. Her heart beating a thousand times a minute, she looked to the left to see her would-be captor yelling and shaking a fist. Then he started to run.

There wasn't much time. In the rearview mirror, she saw the Italian guy come running out of the store, shouting obscenities. You didn't have to understand the language to get the gist of what he was screaming.

As she sped away, she called out, "Sorry!"

Though in her defense, who would leave a gorgeous, low-slung roadster just sitting there running, with the door open, beckoning her? It was if she was meant to borrow the machine.

"Think of it as a hard lesson learned, buddy," she yelled as the car surged forward, her long blonde hair streaming out behind her.

Chapter Ten

June 1330—Ravenskirk Castle, England

Henry couldn't stop staring at the necklace. Why did she say he must hurry home to Ravenskirk? As he walked through the forest, he looked over his shoulder. The woman was nowhere to be seen. Henry let out a breath. The old woman was more than she seemed. As if the bird heard his thoughts, a raven cawed from the trees. Henry crossed himself and laughed at what he had done. Did he really think the woman had turned into a bird and flown away?

One of Henry's knights called out, "We had begun to wonder what happened to you, my lord."

Another leaned forward in the saddle. "You met with the witch of the wood." He crossed himself. "'Tis rumored she is a powerful which. Did she try to steal you away, our lovely lord?"

Henry wanted to laugh but couldn't. He felt uneasy, as if the trees were watching him. The woman had some great power about her, and he would not risk angering her spirit.

"I'm much prettier than the lot of you."

The men chuckled as they made their way home. The day was warm and the men in good spirits as they rode. As they crossed through a small village on the outskirts of his lands, an old, hunched-over woman stood in the road, blocking their way.

"Hold."

"My lord, men came. They stole our livestock." She stood there, wringing her hands.

Henry dismounted. He went to the woman, taking her arm, and gestured to one of his men. "Bring ale."

He led her over to a low stone wall and saw her seated.

"What did these men look like?"

The woman spat. "They wore the colors of Lord Hallsey. Said he was to be our lord now. Is this true, Lord Ravenskirk?"

He cursed viciously. "The whoreson is growing bolder. How dare he send men onto my lands to steal.

"Do not fear, madam. I am your lord. And I will see your livestock returned." He pointed to four of the men. "My knights will guard the village until I have taken care of the threat."

The woman knelt at his feet. "I am most grateful."

Henry pulled her up by the arms. "You are under my protection."

He spoke to the men: "Be aware of your surroundings. If I know Hallsey, he will strike again. Be ready. And send word if anything happens."

Henry tossed one of the knights a bag of coins. "Purchase new livestock and whatever else was taken."

The men nodded as Henry mounted and urged his horse to gallop. He muttered, "I have beaten him in every tourney, and how was I to know 'twas his wife? All women look alike in the dark."

He must've spoken louder than he thought, for his men chuckled and continued making ribald jests the entire way home.

Chapter Eleven

Charlotte lifted one hand off the wheel. Nope, no more shaking. The adrenaline was finally wearing off. She shifted, easing the seat back as far as it would go. The bulk of the backpack made her lean forward. In her haste to flee, she'd left it on, and so far there was nowhere to stop and take it off. The messenger bag dug into her hip as the seatbelt mashed into her side.

A huge sigh of relief coursed through Charlotte. Even with all the commotion, she hadn't lost the two precious bags. But both pairs of boots and the rest of her stuff were still sitting in the hotel. In her bags she had the daggers and her medieval clothing, along with the journal and other odds and ends. Her bracelet sparkled in the sunlight. A glance in the rearview told her she'd gotten away. Charlotte kept close to the coast. At some point, she'd have to find a way to return the car. Apologize for what she'd done. Hope the guy would understand and not press charges.

Twenty-two years and she'd never stolen a thing. Not

even a pack of gum when she was a kid. Charlotte snorted. The Aston Martin was significantly larger than a pack of gum.

But my oh my, could this baby fly. The leather seats enveloped her, and the sound of the engine and the salty air made her want to drive forever. Forget all about some crazy guy wanting to kill her all because of another dead guy.

It was like some video game gone rogue. Charlotte flicked through the stations until she found one playing eighties music. It seemed the DJ was on the same wavelength, as one perfect driving song after another came on. Singing along, Charlotte pressed down on the gas.

Maybe thirty minutes had passed, and the instant she started to relax, a glance in the rearview showed a car coming up fast. She stepped on the gas, laughing as the car surged forward. For a moment she wondered how fast the car could go. Too bad she was running from a killer instead of taking a road trip.

She had to slow down as she took the next curve. Apparently the guy behind her had no such qualms, for he bumped her. The impact jarred her from her teeth to her toes as she fought to keep control of the car.

Thank you, universe, for keeping other cars off the road. Where was everybody? It was a beautiful day and the promenade had been packed. Okay, maybe not a totally clear road. A truck passed her, preventing the man chasing her from hitting her again. She made the mistake of looking over the edge. There was no shoulder, and no guardrail, just a very steep and scary drop-off. Charlotte inched the car over toward the centerline.

As he crept closer to bump her again, Charlotte jammed on the brakes. She watched in slow motion as his car seemed to bounce off the Aston Martin. Saw him frantically trying to gain control as the car started to spin. Helpless, she watched as the car spun off the edge, seeming to hover in the air before it vanished. If someone had asked her, Charlotte couldn't tell them if it was the fireball she saw or the explosion she heard first.

A piece of debris from the car flew up and hit her on the shoulder. "Ouch, damn it."

Charlotte touched her shoulder. Her fingers came away red. Her hand shook on the wheel, blonde hair whipping in the wind, blowing across her face.

She couldn't stop. The authorities would arrest her. Not only to question her about what happened, but for stealing the car. If she failed to go back in time, she'd have a big ole mess to clean up.

As her breathing slowly returned to normal, Charlotte pulled out her phone, tapping the maps app for directions. Once she got to Falconburg Castle, she'd anonymously call and tell them where they could find the car.

Boy oh boy, that guy was gonna be furious when he saw the damage. A piece of banana-yellow plastic flew across the road and skittered over the edge. Charlotte winced. She wouldn't think about how much it would cost to fix the beautiful car.

There were ominous storm clouds gathering above her and still no place to pull over. "Please let there be a turnoff soon." Thunder reverberated through the sky and lightning flashed as the first drops of rain started to fall.

One good thing about going fast? The faster you drove, the less wet you got. Charlotte hit the gas coming out of the curve. It was pouring now and the thunder was getting louder. In the middle of the storm, Charlotte swore she heard the familiar haunting tune. She didn't see the piper anywhere, but she knew it was him.

"My lady, beware!"

Lightning hit the car, surrounding it. Blinding white light filled the vehicle as her body went numb. She felt tingly all over, like her entire body had fallen asleep. Charlotte couldn't feel the wheel; her fingers were numb. The electronics in the car went haywire. It was like driving in a bubble of energy. She hit something in the road and the car started to spin. There was a partial guardrail, and Charlotte prayed it would hold. Sparks flew up around her, mixing with the lightning, and a horrible screeching filled the air as the guardrail gave way.

Charlotte screamed as the car went over the edge. For a moment the car seemed to hover in the air. Then she smelled something burning, heard a crash, and everything went black.

Charlotte came to, choking on seawater. Her fingers desperately worked to free the seatbelt as the car sank deeper and deeper and she was pulled under.

The seatbelt finally came loose, and she swam toward the surface, lungs bursting. When she surfaced, Charlotte found herself in the midst of a terrible storm. Waves crashed over her, sending water up her nose. The salt water made every cut from the accident burn. How had she survived going over the cliff?

She held her hand up and saw the blood. Fear filled her. Out of all the thousands of time she'd swum in the ocean, Charlotte had never worried about sharks. But here, bloody and in the middle of the ocean? She couldn't catch her breath. This was it. Now she'd never find her sisters. It was too late. She was dying. The wind howled and waves crashed over her as Charlotte struggled to take a breath. The certainty she wasn't alone in the water was the last thing she remembered.

They were half a day's ride from Ravenskirk. Out of all his family's estates, it was Henry's favorite. His eldest brother, Edward, lived in the largest castle. Robert was lord over the most ornate estate. Henry teased him that it was too beautiful to be formidable. His youngest brother,

Christian, had the smallest home, yet it controlled a strategic point, its bridge the only access across the river.

Henry thought of his second-eldest brother, John. He felt the loss every day. Once in a while Henry woke in the middle of the night, sure he had heard his brothers laugh. The feeling John was still alive would fill him. Those nights he could not sleep and would pace the battlements until dawn. John's castle was the scariest. 'Twas rumored to be haunted, and Henry wondered if the servants had all fled without their lord there. Mayhap not. Edward would see to it in John's absence. Henry let out a breath. He should visit. Make sure ruffians hadn't invaded.

A raven landed in a tree, pulling him out of his melancholy thoughts. The bird tilted his head at Henry, cawed, took to the air, and cawed again. The black bird flew to another tree, and seemed to look back at him as if to tell him to come along. Talking birds? He was a dolt.

Something unnatural was happening. Henry didn't know why—mayhap 'twas his encounter with the witch in the wood—but something about the bird made him sit up taller in the saddle. He must make haste. The men, sensing his unease, urged the horses to a gallop. Henry didn't know why he must get to the beach, only that the feeling was strong.

"Do you see any wreckage?"

His men dutifully looked to the land and sea for signs of a shipwreck.

"None, my lord."

"Make haste—there is someone washed up on shore."

Two of the men stayed with the horses.

"Bloody hell." He dismounted, running down the curving path to the shore. 'Twas a woman on the beach. He knelt down beside her. Was she dead?

Henry placed a finger under her nose and felt air. She lived.

The girl had beautiful long hair the color of winter wheat, her face deathly pale, lips slightly blue. One of the men jumped back, crossing himself. "She has black legs and white arms—a demon. Where are her clothes?"

Another of the men sounded horrified. "My lord, look at her feet. Her toes. They are blue, like the scales of a fish."

Another of the knights said, "We should leave it. Look at the hump on its back."

Henry rolled his eyes. "'Tis not a hump. 'Tis a pack of some sort. Dolt."

A few of the man nervously laughed. Henry rolled her to one side.

"She is an angel," the man whispered.

"And you have been kicked in the head too many times."

The man was right. The girl had the face of an angel. Her clothing was scandalous. Where was her dress? The angel started to cough and retch, and the men jumped back, crossing themselves.

"'Tis a mermaid."

"Nay, look at the black legs. 'Tis a sea monster washed up."

"Don't be daft," Henry said. "It is a lady washed ashore from a wreck."

One of the men scratched his head. "Then why isn't there

any wreckage or a ship anchored at sea?" He seemed to think about what he said before he bobbed his head and said, "Mayhap she fell from heaven."

Dolts. The lot of them.

Chapter Twelve

Charlotte rolled over, retching until her sides hurt. She was lying in the sand, water lapping at her, and she smelled... horses and men.

Someone was speaking to her. She felt warm hands rubbing her arms. Everything was blurry. But at least she wasn't dead. Charlotte squinted up at the cliff but didn't see any sign of the guardrail. She looked toward the water where the car had sunk. Hope the guy had good insurance. There were voices babbling all around her, but she couldn't make out the words. Once again Charlotte succumbed to darkness.

Slowly she swam toward the surface of consciousness. The sound of men's voices filled the air. Was she back at the camp? Someone had moved her away from the water and she was leaning against rocks, draped in a cloak. She coughed again, spitting up salt water. Her bracelet was gone. She must have lost it during the accident.

A man knelt down in front of her. He was out of focus, so

she was guessing she must've hit her head pretty hard in the accident. Charlotte could hear him talking but couldn't make out the words. A sense of dread filled her as she patted her body for the precious backpack and messenger bag. The bags were shoved into her lap, and she exhaled a huge sigh of relief.

"We mean you no harm, demoiselle. You are safe."

The voice was warm and comforting. Charlotte wanted to open the bags, check the contents, but her hands weren't working properly. She hugged the bags tight as she felt herself falling.

Henry caught the girl as she swooned again. He wanted to move her but was afraid she'd injured her head. They would wait. When she woke again, he would take her home. To Ravenskirk.

He turned her to the side as she retched again. "My lady?" Henry caught sight of her bare feet. "Something is amiss with your feet. The water has turned your toes blue, like the scales of a fish." He made a strangled noise in the back of his throat.

"Norman French, right?" She laughed, the sound tinkling on the air like raindrops on glass. He wanted to hear her laugh again.

"Could you speak regular English, please? And my toes are fine. It's how we decorate them where I'm from. Could you tell me exactly where I am?"

By her speech, she was no noble. She had a strange manner of speaking. He wondered where she was from. She gazed up at him, and Henry lost himself in the clear gray depths. He would not have to look down to speak with her. She was uncommonly tall for a woman.

"Crap on toast. The damn daggers are gone too."

He watched as she opened the strange bags she was carrying. He leaned closer, trying to peer inside.

"Thank the stars, everything else is still here." She looked up at him. "I was afraid I might have lost them, and they are precious to me."

"I understand, lady. My men and I found you washed up on the shore. You seem to have lost your clothes." He pointed to her shapely legs. "We are half a day's ride from Ravenskirk."

"They're in my bag, but I'm afraid they're soaking wet, just like me." She tilted her head at him. "I don't remember a Ravenskirk. Am I close to Falconburg Castle?"

He'd only met James Rivers, Lord Falconburg, a few times. He didn't remember James having any kin.

"Are you related to him?"

"No. But that's where I was going." She sighed. "It's a long story, and I'm wet and itchy."

"He is away for the next fortnight." Henry's brothers were gossips, the lot of them. All his news came from them or travelers. He was content to leave court intrigue behind and spend his days at Ravenskirk.

Henry was shocked he had forsaken his courtly manners. He helped her to her feet, making her a small bow. "I am Henry, Lord Ravenskirk. My men and I will escort you to my home, where you can warm yourself by the fire."

"That will work. A fortnight is two weeks, right?"

Where was she from? "Aye, mistress." Henry took the reins. One of the men had led the horse down to them, so the lady would not have to walk, though he would have gladly carried her. Looking at her, Henry almost wished he could undo his vow never to marry. She was comely, and there was something about her that made him believe she would be the kind of woman to stay by his side forever.

"Can you ride?"

She eyed the horse then him. "I can," she said as she stumbled in his arms.

"Perhaps not yet." Henry lifted her up on the horse. He reached around her to take the reins.

She tilted her head back to look at him. "I know this is going to sound strange, but I'm having a hard time remembering things. I think I hit my head really hard. There's a big bump on the back. What year is it, again?"

She seemed to be holding her breath, as if his answer was uncommonly important. He was curious about her. Enchanted, truth be told.

"'Tis the year of our Lord 1330."

"Oh." She smiled at him, and his heart thumped in his chest. It was as if he could feel the cheerfulness from her body.

"One more question? What month is it?"

He wondered if all her wits were there. But he answered. "June, lady."

"Good. I actually did it," she whispered.

Henry didn't ask her what she meant. A strange feeling went through him, and he remembered the words of the witch he'd encountered in the woods. *A stranger will become more important to you than your own life.*

Perchance she was the one?

Chapter Thirteen

The sand made her itch, and her skin felt tight from the salt water. Charlotte blinked. It wasn't a dream. The men dressed as medieval buffs were still milling around. They blurred, and her head pounded in tune to the waves breaking against the shore.

The wind shifted, carrying the faint smell of sick. Yuck. The memory of barfing up sea water onto the hottie's boots made her wish a wave would pull her back into the ocean.

The sound of a raven silenced the seagulls. When she blinked, the hottie and his twin were kneeling in front of her. "Yowza, are there two of him?"

"'Tis only me, lady."

"I said that out loud, didn't I?"

He chuckled, a deep, throaty sound, warming her to her toes. Talk about handsome as hell.

"I'm sorry about throwing up on your shoes. Weren't we on a horse?"

"Do not worry yourself. The water washed them well

enough." He held out a hand, helping her to her feet. "You were ill again and insisting you needed to wash in the sea. We brought you back down to the shore. Think you are ready to travel?"

"I'm good to go." Charlotte couldn't seem to find her balance.

"I won't let you fall."

His hands were warm and callused. Within his arms Charlotte felt at peace for the first time since she'd lost Lucy.

"I'm grateful for the rescue. I'm Charlotte. Charlotte Merriweather." She swayed and tripped over a rock. "Did you already tell me your name? My head is fuzzy."

"Henry, Lord Ravenskirk, at your service."

He swept her up into his arms as if she were a small kitten. And she wasn't some cute, petite thing.

"Please don't let me be drooling."

"What is drooling?"

This must be what a hot flash felt like. Charlotte was grateful there wasn't a mirror nearby. "I don't know what's wrong with me. I thought I was thinking that in my head, but I guess I said it out loud."

She shook her head. "Drooling is when spit leaks out of your mouth...though drooling sounds much lovelier, don't you think?"

Her rescuer threw his head back and laughed, as did several of the men with him. Could she be any more awkward?

He stared at her mouth, making her swallow. "Nay, lady.

You are not drooling." He looked at her feet. "Did you injure your foot?"

"I think I twisted my ankle. It hurts."

"You will ride with me." He lifted her up onto the horse. Once seated behind her, he put his arms around her to take the reins. No, no, no. She did not have time to get involved with anyone. The only priority was to find her sisters.

Yeah, keep telling yourself that, sugar, the voice in her head mocked. Henry had rugged good looks and seemed strong on the inside as well as outside. The wind blew his hair in her face, and she barely resisted the urge to touch. Charlotte loved the color of her own blonde hair, until she saw his. It looked like he'd spent a fortune having various highlights and lowlights blended through it, when she knew it was from spending a lot of time outside.

She'd actually done it. Elation coursed through her. But how? Did it have something to do with the lightning? Never mind; she had plenty of time to figure it out. Maybe her sisters would have an idea, though did it really matter? It wasn't like anyone else would be coming to join her. And given Lucy and Melinda were still missing, she didn't think you could go back. Seemed like time travel was a one-way ticket. Charlotte refrained from bursting into song. Now she could focus all her energy on finding her sisters. Fingers crossed she was in the same year as them.

"Ravenskirk. Is it yours?" She wasn't a gold digger, not by any means. In fact, she'd prefer a cottage to a castle. But she needed someone with enough power to help her.

"Aye, have we met before?" He spoke close to her ear, his

deep, scratchy voice sending shivers through her. "I would certainly remember meeting one as pleasing as you, demoiselle."

Oh dear, she was in trouble. He was charming as well as handsome. Charlotte looked up at the sky. It was a bright cerulean blue, reminding her of his eyes. She could feel the strong muscles in his legs against her thighs as he guided the horse. Her sodden bags dripped as they rode. Her leggings and t-shirt were already dry.

So many questions. But she couldn't start firing them at him one after another without giving herself away. "How far is your home?" She looked around from side to side. "I don't see a castle, and I would think they're big enough I would notice beforehand."

He chuckled. "Ravenskirk is half a day's ride. My men and I were on our way home when we spied something on the beach. Shipwrecks tend to wash up along these beaches. The rocks are treacherous. Instead of finding the remains of a ship, we found you, lady."

"You don't have to call me lady. It's Charlotte, remember? Charlotte Merriweather."

"As you wish."

She twisted around to look at his face and see if he was mocking her. Nope. He looked serious. The breeze caught a lock of his hair. It was down to the tops of his shoulders, and for a moment she wished hers was short instead of reaching halfway down her back. Between the time in the ocean, lying on the sand, and now this wind, it was going to be an awful mess when she tried to comb all the tangles out.

"Were you traveling by ship, Mistress Merriweather?"

Charlotte fidgeted. Henry seemed like the kind of man she could tell the truth, but she wasn't sure. He also seemed like he didn't take anything in life too seriously. She couldn't say why she thought so, only that it was an impression based on what she'd seen so far. And she needed someone to take her seriously.

"I was in an accident. I found myself washed up on the shore."

Hopefully that would be enough.

"I will send a messenger to your family. Where are you from?"

Great. Just great. Now what was she going to say? Charlotte racked her brain for what she'd written down in her journal. She'd come up with a story and thought it was a good one. The blinding headache was making it hard to focus. *Deep breaths. Calm. Now remember.*

"I'm from a distant land. I don't think you've heard of it. It's called America." She paused to see what he would say. He waited for her to continue.

"I was traveling to England to find my sisters, Lucy and Melinda. My aunt and I haven't had a letter from them in a very long time. I'm not exactly sure where to find them." Which was true.

"Where did they say they were going?"

Before she could answer, one of Henry's men rode up beside them. He was a scary-looking man. She wouldn't want to meet him in a dark alley. Thank the stars he was on their side.

"My lord, we should stop here. The lady needs dry her clothes." He leaned closer to Henry, and if Charlotte hadn't been sitting right in front of him she wouldn't have been able to hear what he said next.

"One of the men spotted a man wearing Hallsey colors."

"Tell the men to stop." Henry looked down at her, and she was struck again by how good-looking he was. She only hoped he was as pretty on the inside as he was on the outside.

"You heard?"

She nodded. "Are we in danger?" She felt his body tense.

"Fear not. You are safe. We will stop and build a fire so you can dry your clothing. Put on something more...er, more. I do not want you to take a chill. There was no chest washed up on shore. You have nothing but your wee bags?"

"I have two dresses, but they're soaking wet. I'll hang them next to the fire to dry." It had never occurred to her to pack the clothes in a waterproof bag. It wasn't like she could have foreseen driving over a cliff into the ocean.

Chapter Fourteen

There was a small clearing in the woods. Henry dismounted, lifting her off the horse.

"You can put me down."

"Nay, your foot is swollen." The last time a guy had carried her was her dad when she was small. It was nice to be taken care of. Charlotte guessed he must be about six foot two. She liked that he was taller than her. He carried her over to a boulder and gently put her down.

"Stay here and rest. My men will build a fire and make sure all is well. I will fetch you something to drink."

She watched him go, admiring his form. He looked healthy and strong. Not like those guys that spent all their time in the gym. Henry looked like he'd worked outside his whole life, doing things with his hands. *Like fighting with swords?* said the snarky voice inside her head.

One of the men started a fire. Charlotte wished she'd paid closer attention. In her pack, she had a pack of waterproof matches, but certainly couldn't bring them out in front of everybody.

While it was a warm day, she was grateful for a fire to dry her things. Everyone was busy, so she opened her backpack and pulled out her clothes. When Charlotte had a few minutes to herself, she'd dump out both bags and check everything over. If she did it now, she had a feeling too many curious eyes would watch. Not to mention she didn't want to be under attack and trying to stuff everything back in the bags. When she stood, her stomach rolled, the pain in her ankle making her pant.

"Lady? May I aid you?"

One of the men took her arm.

"I wanted to look for sticks so I can dry my clothes. A drying rack is easy to make, and I have twine to tie them together."

"Rest, lady. I will gather your sticks."

The man came back with an armful of wood. "Will these do?"

"Yes, thank you."

He handed her each stick and watched as she tied them together, making a drying rack. Then he nodded, took her twine, and made her two more.

"They will be overlarge." Henry handed her a tunic and hose. "You needs dry what you are wearing."

Charlotte tested her ankle. She could hop. An image of the Easter Bunny wearing her clothes popped into her head, making her giggle. She clapped a hand over her mouth.

Henry rolled his eyes and scooped her up. He carried her behind some bushes and set her down.

"I will turn my back. Lean on me as you need." He said over his shoulder, "I will not look."

Charlotte put her hand on his back, then balanced on her good foot. She got the t-shirt off and her leggings down but couldn't step out of them. *Do something. You're standing naked in the woods with possible thieves around and a camp full of men.*

"Um, Henry? Could you lift me and put me down about two feet to the left? I can't step out of my leggings—I mean hose."

He started to turn, and she yelped. "Don't look."

The man chuckled. His hands came around her waist and he went still. The touch of his hands against her skin warmed her. What was he mumbling?

She wished she spoke Norman French. But she gave him credit—he had his eyes closed as he lifted her, turned her, and put her down to his left.

"Better?" he said in a strangled voice.

"Much. Now hold still while I dress." She pulled the tunic over her head. It was a deep blue and beautifully embroidered. When she inhaled, it smelled like him. Then she looked at the hose and let out a sigh.

An answering chuckle told her he knew what she needed.

"Shall I lift you now, lady?"

He didn't give her time to answer before he pulled her against him and lifted her a few inches off the ground. Leaning back against him, Charlotte was able to pull the hose up.

"I'm dressed."

"You look fetching in my tunic and hose."

Their gaze held. Henry picked her up again. "Did you not eat during your journey?"

Her stomach growled in response.

"I thought not. I will feed you, Mistress Merriweather."

In the makeshift camp, sitting on her rock, Charlotte noticed one of the men watching her. She smiled at him and he nodded. As he turned, she saw he had a hand on the hilt of his sword. He must've been assigned to watch her. It made her feel better. Safe.

It seemed like days ago since she'd eaten the fish and chips for lunch, but it had probably only been hours or a day at most. Her stomach protested, telling her she needed to eat now. As if thinking of him conjured him, Henry brought her bread and cheese. Then he handed her a cup. She sniffed. Ale. She wasn't a fan, but it would do.

"I didn't realize how thirsty and hungry I was. Thank you, Lord Ravenskirk."

"You will have a proper meal when we reach my home."

While she finished her meal, she noticed the men were spread out in a circle, all of them seeming to go about their normal business but looking very alert.

She watched, fascinated by everything they did, taking in every detail, from the style of their clothing to the weapons, horses, and the sound of their voices. She knew they were speaking Norman French, and was happy Henry spoke to her in English. How strange she must sound to him. It seemed his men also spoke English—she heard one of them saying it was the language the wenches spoke in the tavern.

She tried not to take offense.

The weather was nice. She guessed it was in the low to mid-sixties. She was looking forward to it cooling down a bit tonight. Tonight she would actually sleep in a castle. When they were settled, she needed to figure out how to get Henry to help her find her sisters. While he was attractive, Charlotte had come to accept she would never marry. It just never seemed to work out for her, no matter how much she wanted to find that one guy. It seemed fate had other plans.

There was a scuffle at the far side of the camp. A screech made her shiver. One of the scary-looking men dragged a body out. Charlotte clapped a hand over her mouth so she wouldn't scream.

"The man was alone. Likely a scout."

Henry examined him.

"'Tis one of Hallsey's men. Liam, Guy. Ride out, see if any of his men are following us."

Charlotte was lightheaded. The man was dead and they were all acting like it was no big deal. *Remember, this is medieval England. Things are different here. They are well within their rights to kill that man. To them it is normal. Get it together.*

She opened her eyes to see blue leggings—no, make that hose; that's what they wore here. *You will not faint, Charlotte Merriweather.*

"I am sorry you had to witness violence. He is one of Lord Hallsey's men. My enemy." He took her hand in his, the calluses on his palm rubbing against her skin.

"Do not worry. I will protect you and keep you safe." And

then he smiled at her, a dazzling grin. "After all, you are much too beautiful for me to allow another to carry you off."

It had the desired effect. Charlotte laughed. "I'm feeling a bit better, thank you."

She wanted to tell him she'd never seen a dead man before. Wanted to tell him she knew what it felt like to stab her knife through a side of beef. But thinking about that made her stomach do flip-flops.

He was definitely the man to help her. Now the only question was to figure out how to find her sisters.

Chapter Fifteen

So many questions he wanted to ask the strange woman. Henry believed her tale of traveling to visit her sisters. He found it more difficult to believe she was the only survivor of a shipwreck with no wreckage. Not a single piece of ship or person washed ashore.

No matter how many tourneys or places he visited, Henry always felt a sense of peace fill him as he clapped eyes on his home.

"Oh my goodness, is that yours?"

"Aye. I am the third of five brothers. My sire provided each of us with a castle. Mine is not the largest, but 'tis home."

She twisted in the saddle to look up at him. "You have four other brothers and you all have castles? Do your parents live in a castle too?"

"They did. They died years ago."

Oblivious to his discomfort, Charlotte looked about as if she had never seen a castle before. Henry had to wonder, where did she come from?

"This is a really long bridge. With the castle sitting in the middle of the water, how do you grow anything?"

"'Tis fresh water. There are two wells inside and a deep pit in the ground for waste. I did not build the castle. It was already complete when I moved in." He shifted in the saddle. Henry knew his father had fought and won Ravenskirk from the Hallseys. They still bore him ill will because of it.

"It's good the waste doesn't go into the fresh water. You can catch diseases that way."

He wondered what she meant by *diseases*, but before he could ask, she said, "You know, things that make you ill."

"There are gardens within the courtyard where we grow food. And many of the people grow food that is brought into the castle like the orchards we rode through. In times of war, the people seek refuge inside the castle walls. We can take apart the bridge."

She leaned over, looking into the water, and he had to pull her back so she didn't fall off the horse.

"How deep is it?"

"'Tis deep enough to swim in. And stocked with fish."

"Your home is very beautiful and forbidding. It's a nice contrast."

He was pleased she found favor with his home. Henry dismounted, lifting Charlotte off the horse. She was too thin. Did her family not have enough? From the fine fabric of her clothes, he thought they were of sufficient means. Perhaps from a minor family. By her speech, she was no peasant. Though not from a noble family either.

"You can put me down. My ankle feels better."

He was loath to let her go.

"If you feel any discomfort, I will carry you inside."

When she smiled, he wanted to stand there forever like a dolt, staring into her gray eyes. As he lowered her to the ground, he heard her sharp intake of breath and lifted her up again.

"Wait. I can walk."

He watched as she took a small step. "I will stay close in case you have need of me."

"Lord Ravenskirk?" A small hand tugged on his tunic. Henry knelt down to face a wee girl. She held up a doll with a rip to its stomach.

"They tortured Dolly." The little girl pointed to two small boys playing with wooden swords. She looked so angry that Henry had to press his lips together so he wouldn't laugh.

"Lads. Come here."

The two boys stood before him, eyes downcast, feet shuffling in the dirt.

"Look at me."

Slowly, they raised their heads to meet his eyes.

"You want to be knights when you grow up?"

They nodded. "Aye, my lord."

"And as a knight you must protect women. Women are to be cherished. Only women can bear children. We must love and protect them always."

The two boys looked abashed.

"Kneel before your lady."

The two boys knelt in the dirt in front of the girl.

"Offer your sword and swear to protect her."

Each boy held out his sword and solemnly said, "I will protect you from all harm, Gilly."

Gilly smiled at the lads. "I accept your vows."

Henry smiled hearing the seriousness in her voice. "Take Dolly in and have one of the women sew her back together. Then have Mrs. Benton give each of you a pastry."

The three children ran off. Henry called out, "Where is Timothy?"

"I saw him running away after Mistress Charlotte arrived. He was babbling about faeries and demons and dark doings."

A raven circled overhead, cawing, and Henry rolled his eyes. Royce, his captain and friend, cursed. "Have a care, Henry. His cousin is a powerful bishop, and she is unprotected without family or kin."

"I will protect her."

"Be careful."

Henry offered Charlotte his arm. "I will show you to your chamber, and then Chester will bring you down to the kitchens for something to eat."

"Thank you again for your hospitality."

"After you've eaten, we'll have speech in my solar."

Charlotte couldn't tell if she was in shock or she'd simply been preparing for so long that she'd accepted her situation. It was amazing to see a living, breathing castle. The inhabitants going about their day-to-day lives, children playing, men practicing with swords.

It seemed like a movie, and yet it felt like home, which she couldn't explain. Not only was she far from the coast, she'd never been to England before. Not in all her travels.

So why did she feel like Ravenskirk was home?

"My lord's chamber is across the hall." Chester, one of Henry's knights, pointed to a wooden door. He opened the door to her room and stood aside to allow her to enter first.

"It's lovely."

"'Tis the nicest chamber in the castle, after my lord's."

The room was beautifully done, the bed huge and heavy looking, with what looked like a soft featherbed on top of the straw, along with decent sheets and blankets.

As she stood in front of the hearth, he said, "There is always a fire, as the rooms are cold all year long, lady."

How did you tell someone, *Hey, I'm from the future*, without sounding totally loony tunes? In her opinion, it would be best to wait until she knew Henry better and he knew she was of sound mind.

There was a pipe sticking out of the wall. Chester saw her looking at it.

"Running water." He pointed to a pitcher and basin. "To wash."

"How clever." She let the water flow into the pitcher.

There was a ceramic cup, and she poured the water into it. It tasted clean, reminding her of well water. A friend of hers in the country was on well water, and Charlotte had always liked the taste.

From the window, she could see the castle reflected in the water surrounding it. The land beyond was green and lush. So many shades of green.

A knock sounded at the door.

"Come in."

A young girl, around eleven or twelve, grinned at her.

"Mistress, I've been sent to fetch your clothes so they can be washed. My lord said you'd been in the sea."

"I leave you in good hands, lady," Chester said, and tweaked the girl's braid as he left.

The girl held out a bundle. "You can wear these while your clothes are cleaned."

Charlotte took the dress from her. It was a pretty dark blue wool, embroidered all around the neckline, sleeves, and hem with what she thought might be bluebells. The chemise was embroidered with leaves.

The girl moved behind her. "I'll assist you, lady."

"Please, call me Charlotte. What's your name?"

"Addie, lady."

"It's a lovely name." She let the girl help her undress.

"You have such beautiful skin. Your hair is so lovely, almost as comely as Lord Ravenskirk's." The girl clapped a hand to her mouth and blushed.

Charlotte knew the feeling well. She also had a bit of a crush on the lord of the castle.

"He's very handsome, isn't he? And you're right, his hair is beautiful." The little girl smiled shyly. Charlotte opened her backpack, taking out the salt-encrusted clothing.

"I hope they will come clean."

The girl looked at the dresses. "My mum has soap. The clothes will clean."

Charlotte smiled at the girl. "Might your mom have something for the leather on my bags?" She pointed to the salt stains.

While Addie folded up her clothes, Charlotte dumped the contents of the bags on the bed and threw the covers over them. She wondered again why the daggers and bracelet were missing. The daggers couldn't have slipped out—the backpack and messenger bag were both zipped shut. The bracelet fit close to her wrist. She paused. Did they disappear because they didn't yet exist in this time?

"Mistress?

"Sorry, what?"

"I'll bring a bit of soap for you as soon as I take your clothes to be washed." She turned back to Charlotte. "Unless you would like to come with me? I can take you to the kitchens for something to eat. Chester doesn't like to be inside waiting on ladies."

"Lead the way."

As the girl left the room, Charlotte hesitated. "I'll be right there."

She scooped up her stuff and put it in the chest at the foot of the bed. It made her nervous to leave it there, but she'd have to trust no one would go through her things.

Charlotte followed Addie out of the chamber. In the hallway, Chester leaned against the wall.

Addie said, "I'll take Mistress Charlotte to the kitchens for something to eat."

He nodded. "I'll come and fetch you when he wishes to speak with you."

Charlotte followed the girl down to the kitchen, listening to her chatter the entire way. The soft leather shoes she'd been given to wear fit okay, but she longed for her boots. They were currently back in her hotel room. Oh well. She hoped someone would enjoy them. The money and gems were tied in scarves, and now sat in the trunk as well.

As they came into the kitchen, Charlotte smiled. A kitchen was a kitchen, no matter what century you found yourself in.

Chapter Sixteen

Henry looked up from the desk to see Addie and Mistress Merriweather entering the solar. "Feeling better after you've eaten?"

"Much better. Thank you for your hospitality."

He wondered if it had been merely the effects of rescuing a damsel in distress. But no, Henry looked upon her glorious face again. Her long blonde hair hung to the middle of her back, loose around her face. Clear gray eyes gazed at him, and in that moment he knew would do anything in his power to aid her.

"Please sit."

Addie poured them both a cup of wine before scampering out the door. He leaned back in his chair and steepled his fingers underneath his chin. "Tell me again about your sisters, their husbands, and anything you think would be useful in finding them."

He watched as she hesitated for a moment. And Henry wondered what secrets she was keeping. Women always kept secrets. Most benign, but others harmful. He'd run into his share of jealous women who only wanted to make their husbands angry. Henry had found himself at the end of a blade more times than he cared for. He never meant any harm; he simply adored women. Women of all shapes and sizes. He found beauty in each one. From the tilt of a head, to the sound of laughter, to the way a woman smelled, Henry found all of them enchanting.

Charlotte was the kind of woman to marry, not dally with. Regret filled Henry as he thought of never kissing her full lips. Never caressing her hair, or seeing if her curves were as lush underneath her clothes. He knew if he kissed her once, he'd never want to stop, and that was not acceptable. He pulled his attention back to her.

"I really don't know much. We lost touch." She turned her head and gazed out the window, silent for a few moments.

"I lost touch with Lucy first. It's been a year since I spoke to her. It's been over four months since I heard from Melinda."

Charlotte drank her wine. He thought she looked forlorn. And Henry's heart went out to her.

"Were you angry with each other?" He remembered throughout his entire childhood his parents always shouting at one another. Henry swore they never spoke a pleasant word in all the years they were married. They were both gone, and it pained him to say he did not miss either of them. Perhaps they had found peace in the next life.

"No, we're close to each other. But when you're so far

away, it's difficult. Letters take ages, if they reach the intended party at all. I haven't heard from either of them in a long time, so you can imagine how worried I am. It's why I finally decided to make the journey."

"What do you know about their husbands, or where they live? Surely they spoke of their homes in the letters they sent?"

He watched her. When Charlotte Merriweather wasn't telling the truth, she looked up and to the right. To his surprise, he noticed every detail about her. While he admired women and loved them, they were all rather interchangeable. Talking about court fashions and gossip, having babies, and scolding. But her...something was different about this woman, from her speech and manners to the very air that surrounded her. Mayhap 'twas her coming from another country.

"Lucy is married with children, but I don't know her husband's name. I think she lives near Blackford. Do you know it?"

"Blackford Castle is across the country on the west coast. Lord Blackford is a fearsome warrior and kin to my family. A distant cousin. My oldest brother, Edward, is a terrible gossip. I will send a messenger to find out what he knows."

Charlotte paced back and forth across the room, stopping to pick up a book or object that caught her eye. She seemed restless. How would he fare if he'd traveled such a long distance and could not find his brothers? They were all close, and he couldn't imagine being without them.

"Lucy's different, like me. She should stand out. And she

talks like me. She's twenty-four, with long brown hair and blue eyes. The middle sister. I would greatly appreciate any information that your brother or cousin might have."

"Tell me about your other sister." He couldn't keep the disbelief out of his voice. "Perchance you know her husband's name or where she lives?"

Again Charlotte looked up and to the right. What reason did she have to be untruthful? Was she afraid of something? Had she run away from a husband who beat her? And at that thought, a pang went through him. For while he could not marry her, he did not want her to be married. He was a fool.

"Melinda is my oldest sister. She's kinda bossy. Twenty-six, with green eyes and long, curly red hair. She went—well, the last I heard, she was at Falconburg."

"Falconburg Castle is two days' ride. I will dispatch another messenger. One of my brothers told me Lord Falconburg married a beautiful woman with red hair a few years ago."

"She's only been gone four months or so. No way it could be her...at least I don't think so. Though Falconburg was the last place I know she went. I need to get there and ask if anyone knows her."

"We must take care. There is sickness about. People are struck with a fever, then die a few days later. Some of the villagers believe the devil is walking about. 'Tis dangerous to travel unless necessary."

Charlotte bit her lip. "I'll wait to hear what your messengers find. But I will have to travel to Falconburg and

Blackford to search for them. It's the reason I'm here."

"And I will send an escort with you as soon as 'tis safe. Lord Falconburg, James, is not hospitable to visitors. I will send a messenger first, and once we have word, we can make the journey if the sickness has passed from the lands."

Henry held up a hand. He didn't want her to get her hopes up. "If your sister has only been gone four months, she cannot be Lady Falconburg, don't you agree? Wouldn't you know if your sister married a noble? And an extremely rich noble at that?"

She wouldn't meet his eyes. And instead of asking her outright why she was lying to him, he decided he would uncover what he could about her himself.

"It is possible, though. Given the way I haven't received any letters lately, it's possible Melinda married and I don't know about it. Will you help me?"

While Henry was thinking about the probability of her sisters being married to James and William, he heard a raven call in the distance. The hair on the back of his neck stood up. He'd heard many ravens throughout his life. But now the birds seemed to appear when Mistress Merriweather was near. Or when the old woman from the wood was close. While Henry would never say it out loud, he swore the bird led him to find her on the beach. Something otherworldly was happening. And the old woman's message ran through him.

Those you call friend will turn against you. A stranger will become more important to you than your own life. And when you see nothing but darkness ahead, look to the east.

"Aye. I will send messengers. We will find your sisters." He stood and made her a low bow. "After all, I am a knight and sworn to aid those in need."

Was Charlotte the stranger? If the old woman's prophecy were true, which friend would turn against him? And even more alarming was her prediction about a coming darkness. By the east, did she mean one of his brothers would come to his aid? Henry snorted.

Or did she perhaps mean William Brandon and his army? It made his head ache, and Henry was tired of thinking about it. He needed to ride.

"Thank you again, Lord Ravenskirk. I have imposed on your hospitality for too long. Is there someone who could take me to a nearby inn where I can wait to hear back from your messengers?"

"Nonsense. You shall stay here at the castle, where it is safe. And then I will not have to search you out when the messengers return." He walked to the door and opened it. "Would you like to join me for a ride? It's a lovely day."

Chapter Seventeen

"My lord, come quickly."

Charlotte looked up, hearing the alarm in the man's voice. Henry was already on his feet, calling out over his shoulder, "Stay here until I know 'tis safe."

Well, that wouldn't do. She was from a family of curious women. Charlotte packed up the makeshift picnic, made her way down from the battlements, and dropped everything off in the kitchens before going outside. They'd spent the entire past week together.

The activities served as a distraction from endlessly asking when the messengers would return. He hadn't said, but she thought Henry was concerned too. They should have been back by now. She hoped they hadn't caught whatever illness was going around.

Henry had taken her on rides to see his lands and meet his people, but only after he'd sent men first to make sure no one was sick. He'd provided dancing and singing at night in the great hall and spent afternoons in the solar with her.

Sometimes they read or talked or simply sat, enjoying each other's company. He was charming and fun to be around.

Now, sugar, you know you like the boy. She rolled her eyes. Why couldn't she have heard Aunt Pittypat's voice in her head when she was lying about her sisters to Henry?

"Is aught amiss, mistress?" Little Addie trembled in the corner.

Charlotte knelt down beside her. "Don't worry, sweetie. I'll find out what's happening. If it were something bad we would have heard all the men shouting and running around."

The girl looked doubtful, but wiped her eyes. "As you say."

"I'll be right back."

She went outside to see what was happening. There was a man lying in the back of a wagon, not moving. It was Liam, one of Henry's knights.

"What happened?"

Henry looked furious. "Lord Hallsey attacked the village again. Burnt it to the ground. Liam managed to cut down three of the men. They were wearing Hallsey's colors."

"He needs stitches in that arm." She looked away from the blood and around the courtyard.

"Aye, I'll see to him. I'm good with a needle and thread." One of the girls eyed Liam as if he were her next needlepoint project, and Charlotte winced. Poor guy wasn't going to get a shot to numb him before the stitching started. Her stomach turned over from thinking of the needle going in and out of his flesh.

"Are you unwell?" Henry took her arm, frowning.

"I'm fine. Just thinking about how the stitches will hurt."

He scoffed. "Hear that, Liam? The lady is worried you're going to cry like a babe."

She wanted to smack him.

"'Tis naught but a scratch, mistress. Don't worry your comely head. Though a kiss might help."

"She'll not be kissing one ugly as you, man. There'll be no kissing. No stealing longing glances either."

Hmm, he sounded jealous. Charlotte grinned. In the short time she'd been here, she'd gone from a full-on crush to seriously liking Henry. Maybe he liked her too. She wanted to skip around the courtyard singing, but then the people would think she was stranger than they already did. A giggle slipped out.

Henry raised a brow, but she shook her head. The men pulled Liam out of the cart. There was a horrible gash across his thigh and another on his back. The smell of something salty and meaty filled the air as they passed by her. She reeled back. It was one thing to see a wound, but to smell it as well was a bit more than she could handle. Charlotte gagged.

The girl who would stitch up Liam followed the men, barking orders.

"Excuse me?"

The girl turned.

"You will clean the wound with alcohol before stitching him up, right?"

"Are you a healer, mistress?"

"No, but I know a bit about injuries. The alcohol will prevent foul humors from entering the body. You pass the needle through fire and then dip it in the alcohol, and pray for fast healing. Then wrap the wounds with clean bandages."

She realized everyone had stopped what they were doing to listen. Charlotte made sure not to say *germs*, since no one would know what they were. Had she said something wrong?

The girl slowly nodded. "A few years back, a healer passed through, said he learned about using alcohol from a healer to the east. Thank ye."

Henry patted her shoulder. "You are a kind woman." He stared at her and Charlotte fought the urge to fidget. "Yet unused to seeing injured men. Your sire kept you locked away?"

"No, I just don't like the sight of blood."

He was about to say something else when another rider appeared. The man was covered in mud, as was the horse.

"The villagers are making their way here, my lord."

"We must make ready."

Charlotte stood in awe as he barked out orders left and right. Someone bumped into her.

"Henry?"

"Aye?"

"I'm good at sorting people out. Can I help with everyone arriving? I'd like to keep busy. It will keep my mind off wondering when the messengers will return."

"If any of the villagers have the sickness, you must not let them stay." He brushed a lock of hair that had come loose from her braid behind her ear. His fingertip brushed her cheek.

"What do I do with them?"

"Tell the man I send with you. He will send them to make camp outside the walls. And mistress?"

She turned to him.

"The messengers will return any day. Do not worry. I said I will aid you in your quest to find your sisters, and I will do everything in my power to find them. I know how important family is."

Could he be any more perfect? She knew there was no Lady Ravenskirk, but did he have a girlfriend? 'Cause if not, Charlotte decided she wanted to apply for the job.

"Everyone, over here. If you're part of a family, stand over here to my right with your family. The rest of you move to my left."

There were people everywhere. From babes to old folks to dogs and livestock.

"Animals go to the barn. The boys will see them fed and cared for." Charlotte dusted her hands off on her dress.

A small hand tugged at her skirts. "Mistress? My lord thought you might be thirsty." The boy held up a glass.

She could smell the fruity wine. "I am parched. Thank you. Could you tell Mrs. Benton I'm going to start sending families into the great hall for supper?"

"Yes, lady." He smiled and disappeared into the crowd.

Charlotte tried to get everyone's attention a few more times, but with at least a hundred people in the courtyard it was no use. So she stuck her fingers in her mouth and let out an ear-piercing whistle.

The courtyard fell silent. She clapped her hands together. "Right. Those with families go to the great hall for supper. Stay together. The rest of you follow them in. Tonight families with children will sleep in the hall. Once it is full, we have room in the chapel and other buildings."

Thank goodness no one showed signs of the sickness. She'd have felt awful turning them away when they had no place to go. Dust filled the air as people traipsed inside the castle. Charlotte drained her cup.

"Where did you learn to do that, lady?" A small boy looked up at her as if she'd conjured dragons out of thin air.

Another frowned. "Ladies shouldn't make such loud noises."

She giggled. "I learned it from a boy when I was about your age. Would you like me to show you?"

The five boys nodded. Charlotte smirked. "Go help in the kitchens. Do whatever is asked of you. After the musicians finish playing, help put away the tables and benches. Then tomorrow I'll teach you to whistle like me."

They huddled together, whispering. The tallest one with black hair and green eyes stepped forward. He held out a hand. "Do we have your word?"

Charlotte spat into her palm, held it out to him, and grinned. "Aye. Do I have yours?"

A huge smile broke out on the boy's face. He spat into his hand and shook. The other four boys did the same. She waited until they'd wandered away before wiping her palm on her skirts. She'd seen the men and boys spit and shake and knew it would carry weight with the boys, but talk about disgusting.

"Foul wench. You are a woman. Not a man. How dare ye act like a man. Giving orders and raising your voice. Women should be silent." Timothy's eyes blazed.

She'd seen that look on religious zealots before. Had come in contact with enough of them during her travels to know how dangerous they could be. Graciousness and a sense of humor usually worked.

"Timothy. How lovely to see you. Would you escort me in to supper?"

He crossed himself. "Nay. You are a demon. I must go to the chapel and pray for your immortal soul."

"Thank you. I can use all the prayers I can get."

He looked horrified as he ran for the chapel. He was really going to be mad when she filled it with people tonight. They needed every inch of space, and the chapel would fit a good forty or fifty people. If he fussed, she'd tell him it was the displaced villagers or their livestock. She'd make sure to speak to Henry about him too. Charlotte didn't want to wake up to find herself tied to a stake and Timothy gleefully throwing the first torch.

Chapter Eighteen

Charlotte stopped in the kitchens to speak to Mrs. Benton. She'd seen Timothy huddled together with three other men, likely telling them of the evils of the female sex after he'd finished praying.

"Do we have enough food and drink for everyone for the next month? I'm guessing it will take that long to start rebuilding the village."

The plump woman looked up at her, a frizzy brown curl escaping from her cap.

"Aye. Ravenskirk boasts a large wine cellar." The woman snorted. "Likely more than Lord Ravenskirk and all his knights could ever drink. His father was a great lover of drink and made sure there was always more than enough."

She wiped her hands on her apron and gestured for Charlotte to sit down. The woman poured them ale. Since she'd been in the past, she swore she'd drunk more than she had in her entire life combined. But though she drank a great deal, she never found herself drunk. Well, except sometimes at supper. When the musicians played and she danced, she found she might drink a bit much and be tipsy by the end of the night.

The cook handed her a piece of bread spread with butter. "And the food? Do we have enough? What about this winter?"

"We have a large larder; do not worry yourself. The lord has always been worried about siege. We will last through the summer, the winter, and to next spring."

"A siege? Is that possible?" Charlotte didn't consider herself claustrophobic by any means, but knowing that she was in the castle sitting in the middle of the water with no way out made her nervous.

"Don't worry, love. Ravenskirk has never been besieged in all the time I've served here. A score of years. I served the lord's sire before he passed and left the castle to young Henry."

"What were his parents like?"

Mrs. Benton frowned. "His lady never stayed here. She preferred to spend her time at court. They were rarely together, and when they were..." The woman looked around, but everyone was so busy going about the task of feeding everyone, no one was paying them any attention.

"How they screamed at each other. They hated each other." She leaned across the table, and Charlotte found herself doing the same. "'Tis a wonder they managed to have five boys." She waggled her eyebrows. "But 'tis said hate and love are two sides of the same coin. Perhaps they came together in the bedroom, or mayhap they liked to continue the fight there." The woman slapped her thighs and laughed.

"Was the marriage arranged?"

"Aye. As most noble marriages are. He had a title and a great deal of land. Her family had a great deal of money." The woman shrugged. "'Tis the way of the nobles."

And Charlotte had to wonder—would Henry marry a noblewoman? She was a nobody. Would he even consider someone like her? She mentally smacked herself. First she had to find her sisters. Then she might consider staying here with Henry...if he even wanted her to.

Supper was a lively affair. Though with so many people, it was stifling in the hall. It was the first time since traveling to the past that Charlotte had found herself hot and sweaty.

Henry made sure she had the choicest bits from the platter as it was passed around. He was always refilling her glass, and seemed to know what she needed before she asked. He had an easy smile and laugh for everyone. She'd noticed more than one serving girl and woman from the village giving him the eye.

The musicians tuned up, and as the final plates were cleared away, Charlotte stood to help move the tables and benches back against the wall.

"Nay, lady. Leave it to the servants." Henry stopped her with a hand on her arm.

"Really, I don't mind. I don't think I'm above anyone else."

He looked at her, a strange look on his face. "I have known many women, and none of them would do half the things you have done since arriving. Chester said I should put you in command of my army the way you sorted everyone in the courtyard today. I am most grateful."

She felt the heat go to her cheeks and hoped she wasn't blushing. By the twinkle in his eye, though, she knew she must be. He bowed to her. "Dance with me?"

"I'm afraid I don't know the dances."

Henry smiled. "Will you allow me to lead, my lady? For I am sure one as graceful as yourself will float on air."

"My sister Lucy had a favorite saying. She liked to say a man was so charming he could beguile an alligator into becoming a vegetarian. I think she must've been thinking of you." She grinned at him.

Henry pursed his lips. "Alligator?"

"You know, like a crocodile."

"Aye. I know about crocodiles. 'Tis rumored one of my brothers wanted to have them sent over from a faraway land and put in his moat. But alas, it is too cold in England for the beasts." He fiddled with his sleeve. "Vegetarian?"

Charlotte mentally cursed. She was trying so hard not to introduce any new words or ideas, but every now and then something slipped out. It was funny—you didn't think about what you said or knew to be common knowledge until you were thrust into a situation that was completely different.

"Vegetarian means a person or animal who does not eat meat."

She watched his lips move as he replayed what she said, and saw when he got it. Henry threw back his head and laughed, the candlelight making the highlights in his hair shine. His laugh was deep and rich and warmed her from the inside out. He led her out to the dance floor and Charlotte lost track of time.

Henry finished seeing to the needs of his men and the villagers under his care. He checked the larder to reassure himself it was sufficiently stocked. He'd never known a day of hunger even through the years of famine. His family had an obsessive need to store food and drink for lean times.

It was late as he strode into the kitchen. Here, though, no one would sleep. There were too many mouths to feed. He found the cook and spoke quietly to her.

"How are the girls and lads I sent to help doing?"

"They'll do just fine. I thank ye for the help." Mrs. Benton pointed to Charlotte. "She is different from other ladies of the court. After she saw all the villagers settled in the hall and the chapel, she helped some of the children with their tasks in the kitchen. She shall make someone a fine wife.

Perhaps someone we know."

Henry wisely kept his mouth shut. Those under his care seemed to think it was their duty to find him a wife. No matter how much he protested, they insisted he needed to be married and provide an heir. Only Royce knew of his vow.

Charlotte sat at the table, her face resting against a platter, sound asleep, a glass of wine still in her hand.

He reached out and stroked her hair. She mumbled something he couldn't understand.

"Charlotte. Wake up."

She grumbled in her sleep but did not wake. Henry picked her up. She wrapped her arms around his neck and sighed. She was tall for a woman, yet so thin. He looked to the cook. "Make sure she eats, Mrs. Benton."

The woman beamed at him, and Henry knew she would be matchmaking. He carried Charlotte through the hall, stepping over bodies, and up the stairs. When he reached her chamber, he shifted her to open the door and she stirred.

"Five more minutes."

Her eyes fluttered open and she blinked at him. "What time is it? Is it morning already?"

Henry looked down at her, feeling something in the air shift. She was beautiful and kind to everyone she encountered. She was willing to do whatever was needed for his people without complaint. Indeed, she would make someone a fine wife. Henry didn't want her to be anyone else's wife.

Mayhap he should speak with the priest about his vow. Was it possible? Could he have a marriage different from his parents? Might two people who cared for each other continue to care for each other as they spent their lives together?

"'Tis late. Go to sleep."

She kissed him on the cheek and closed her eyes. Henry almost dropped her. He heard the sound of a throat clearing, and turned.

His captain stood there, a smirk on his face. Henry scowled at Royce. He would pay the man back in the lists tomorrow. He carried Charlotte over to the bed, gently laid her down, and smoothed the hair back from her brow.

He found he wanted to kiss her, but wouldn't dare with Royce watching.

Henry closed the door softly behind him, thinking of the angel asleep on the other side of the door.

Chapter Nineteen

The next several days passed in a blur. Charlotte was busy helping Henry deal with the villagers' needs. Every day she looked in the larder and wandered through the storage room holding the wine and drink. It was her form of meditation. Seeing the food and drink made her feel like everything would be okay. After all, it wasn't like there was a grocery store down the street if she needed something.

Charlotte was so full after lunch. She and Henry took a walk outside the castle. The open space and lack of people allowed her to reset and enjoy the day instead of worrying all the time.

"What will you do about the village, tell the king?"

"Nay, he is occupied with the sickness spreading across the lands. I will deal with Hallsey myself. He wants my land, has wanted it since before I was born. But he will not have it." Henry squirmed, and she wondered what he wasn't telling her.

"Why does this Lord Hallsey hate you? Did you ravish his

daughter or something?" she teased him.

At the look on his face, Charlotte wanted the ground to open and swallow her up. Her embarrassment was quickly followed by anger. She knew men of this time weren't monks, but she thought he was some kind of Prince Charming and above womanizing.

"You did, didn't you?"

"I was at court. Young and a dolt. In truth, I did not know the lady was Lord Hallsey's wife. She came to me, followed me about. One night I entered my chambers to find her in my bed." He stopped, his face red.

"Afterwards, she went to her husband, told him what she had done. The man has bastards by half the serving women in his keep. He had always been jealous of my family. But after that, he hated me. Swore revenge."

As they came to the bridge, they stopped. The water surrounding the castle was still. Charlotte could see their reflections. The landscape was green and lush, a beautiful location. The castle itself was breathtaking, built in a square with round towers at each point. She could see why someone would choose this spot to build a home.

"I can see why he would be angry, but in your defense you didn't know who she was. She did it to spite him, not because you meant anything to her."

"You wound me."

"Your pride can take it."

Henry blinked at her several times. Then he smiled, and it lit up his entire face. Talk about movie star looks. He held out his arm.

"I know you've been worried about supplies. Have you visited the wells?"

Great, another location to add to her morning rounds. Why hadn't she thought of it before? Right, because she took fresh water for granted, though that was quickly changing.

"No. I wondered what you did for fresh water. I thought you simply dipped the bucket into the water surrounding the castle."

Charlotte's anger quickly dissipated. She didn't know him before she'd arrived. Everyone had a past; she had one herself. What mattered was how Henry behaved now. She had not seen him with another woman. He hadn't even flirted with anyone. Not that they were a couple, but if they became one...well, she would judge him on his actions, not his past deeds.

She'd watched too many relationships end up broken and smashed against the rocks because one person or the other couldn't accept their partner's past. She'd sworn long ago to never be like that.

"There are two freshwater wells. My sire's father was besieged several times and swore he would never run out of water. One of his childhood friends had been besieged, and everyone inside starved and died from lack of water. That is why I have an abundance of food and why my sire did."

He led her through the hall. They stopped to speak with several people. While it hadn't exactly been easy living in the past, it also hadn't been as hard as Charlotte thought it might be. All that time spent in third world countries must've prepared her better than she thought.

The interior of the castle was beautifully furnished with rugs and tapestries on the walls. She'd expected gray stone, but the walls were painted white, and other rooms were beautifully paneled. When she'd asked him about the decorations, Henry said it was considered very modern.

She thought whoever came up with the idea to build a castle in the middle of the water had a great idea. It would be difficult for anyone trying to attack when the owner could simply dismantle the bridge. Of course, she wondered, how did you get out once the enemy left? Did you have another bridge stored away someplace in the castle?

She peered into the well, feeling the cold stone ledge seep into her hands. "How deep is it?"

"No one knows. But we've never run dry. Not from either well." He peered into the water beside her. Their faces reflected back at them. Something glinted at his neck and she turned to him.

As she was about to ask him about it, he got a funny look on his face.

"Did I tell you how I helped an old woman in the woods near where I found you? Some say she's a witch. Others call her a healer. I was returning her necklace to her, but she told me I would know who it was meant for. Perchance you think I'm daft, but I believe it was meant for you."

Henry pulled the necklace out from his tunic and over his head.

Charlotte gasped. "Melinda's favorite necklace."

"Your sister? I thought she was a score and six?" He

dropped the necklace into her hand.

"She is. I wonder how the old woman came by the necklace? Melinda would not have easily given it away. It belonged to our Aunt Pittypat. It was the only possession Mellie had of hers."

Henry took her hand in his. Charlotte felt the calluses on his palm as he stroked the back of her hand.

"I was powerfully drawn to it, and the woman seemed to sense it when she gave it to me. Now we know your sister is somewhere in England."

"But neither messenger found anything. I could slap your brother for sending the messenger on to do his errands instead of sending him back here. I hate waiting."

Henry frowned. "Lady Blackford is old enough to be your dam. And with James away and his wife unwell, we have only the word of the man the messenger spoke with. He said Lady Falconburg has only one sister. With the sickness near, we cannot risk a visit yet."

Was it possible her sisters were being extra careful, trying not to arouse suspicion? But surely they would know if someone was asking that she must be here. Here in medieval England and looking for them. And if that were true, surely they would have come to see for themselves. It was so damned annoying to be so close and yet so very far from finding them.

He pulled her close, as if he knew her thoughts. "We will find them." He looked down at her, ran his fingers through her hair. Charlotte wondered if he was finally going to kiss her. As Henry leaned close enough she could smell the parsley on his breath, she sucked in a breath.

"Pardon, my lord?"

Charlotte wanted to stamp her foot and scream. Talk about terrible timing. Henry seemed to feel the same, by the look on his face. But he pasted on a smile and turned to the garrison knight.

"Aye?"

"There is a dispute over the chickens. You should make haste."

"Bloody hell." He turned to her. "We shall resume speech at supper. Save me a dance or two?"

Heat flooded her face as she clutched the precious necklace in her hand. "All of them."

Chapter Twenty

As Henry left to deal with whatever required his attention, Charlotte thought about her life thus far. She looked down and turned the charms on the necklace over and over again. She didn't believe in coincidence. Somehow there was a connection between the old gypsy woman and the old woman Henry met in the wood.

Magic. Reincarnation. Or something else unexplainable. To hold Melinda's necklace in her hand made Charlotte want to jump in a car and drive. To sing at the top of her lungs. It just wasn't the same on a horse. For one thing, the horse tended to twitch his ears to show his displeasure. Everyone's a critic.

The necklace proved she was in the right time and place. She could quit worrying if she'd made it to the right year. It also told her Melinda wasn't too far away. And if her sister was near, Charlotte had to trust Lucy was also here.

"All women are creatures of evil."

"Timothy. You startled me. What were you saying?"

Great. The wacko was back.

He crossed himself. "Begone, demon." He grabbed her by the arms, shaking her.

Charlotte had just about enough of this deranged loser. She pushed down hard on the nerve between Timothy's neck and shoulder, making him let go of her. She stepped back, standing next to the well.

"You need to leave. Now."

Timothy lunged for her. She held up her hands in defense and realized her mistake as he grabbed for the necklace.

"No!"

In the struggle, the chain broke in two. He held it up, the pupils of his eyes huge. "Unicorns are signs of faeries. Everyone knows fairies are in league with the devil."

Charlotte crossed her fingers behind her back. "My necklace is not evil. It was blessed by the Pope." Technically it was blessed. Aunt Pittypat wore it when she attended mass over Easter in St. Peter's Square, years ago. The Pope gave his blessing, so the necklace was blessed.

Timothy's face turned a pretty shade of eggplant. And she couldn't resist adding, "The necklace also brings good fortune. Now give it back."

He shook the necklace at her. "These heathen charms prove you are a demon. I will take this to my bishop. You will burn."

Timothy drew himself up, shaking his fist in the air, and all at once, as if someone had pried his fingers open, the necklace went flying.

Charlotte watched helplessly as it flew through the air. She jumped, grabbing for it, but it was too late. It went into the well. As she looked over the edge, she watched it hit the water with a splash.

"How could you do something so mean? It was the only thing I had left of my sister. You're a horrible person."

He made more signs at her and retreated. Though not before calling out, "My bishop will hear of this, witch. You will wish you had never come to Ravenskirk."

And for the first time since she'd traveled through time, tears started to fall. Charlotte leaned over the edge of the well, staring at her reflection until the water rippled and blurred.

"My lord?" Chester stood before him. Henry re-sheathed his sword and wondered what he would have to deal with next. Pigs in his bedchamber? Children daring one another to swim in the moat?

"What's happened?"

"I saw Timothy leaving the castle. He was muttering about witches and unicorns." The man looked nervous, and Henry felt like he had eaten bad eels.

"Did he say where he was going?"

"I saw Mistress Merriweather. She was weeping."

"What did he do to her?" Henry bellowed.

Chester sighed. "You know he believes women are evil. He told our lady she was a witch and a demon." Chester scratched his nose. "I'm not certain you could be both."

Henry tried not to laugh, as Chester seemed to be seriously pondering the question.

"Charlotte is neither. Did he hurt her?" If he had, Henry would kill him. He would not tolerate anyone ill-using a woman.

"No. But he took her necklace. The one the old woman gave you. There was a struggle and it went into the well. I tried to help her get it back, but the well is too deep. She was inconsolable. Said it was the only thing she had of her sister. I thought her sister was here in England?"

"She hasn't seen her in a very long time. You know women and their womanly emotions." Henry wasn't about to voice what he suspected. That Charlotte was indeed from a faraway country. He only hoped she wasn't really a faerie. Not that he believed in otherworldly doings.

"He will go to the bishop. The corrupt man would like nothing more than to see my lands and gold confiscated."

Henry's captain clapped him on the shoulder. "Shall we send men after him?"

"No. He is cousin to the bishop. We must tread carefully. Inform me immediately when he returns." Just what Henry needed, another problem to deal with.

Chester left and Royce still stood there, a frown on his face. Henry needed to find Charlotte. Soothe her tender heart.

"You think I should go after him? His claim is ridiculous. Surely the bishop will not listen."

Royce grunted. "I think you will wish you did when he returns."

Chapter Twenty-One

A few days later, Henry watched Charlotte as she talked with the villagers. He was drawn to her. Found himself seeking her out during the day. She came to the lists every morning to watch him train. The men teased him mercilessly.

"My lord? Timothy is back. He's asking to speak with you."

Henry slumped. This would not be good news. "Bring him to my solar."

Henry stopped in front of Charlotte. "You heard?"

She nodded. "He hates me."

"As a favor to a friend of my mothers, I took Timothy as one of my men. He has always believed women to be weak. But lately..." Henry sighed. "He has grown mad. I will deal with him."

He found Timothy in the kitchens terrorizing the girls as they worked. "To my solar."

The man's eyes gleamed with an unholy light. "I come

from a most important meeting with the bishop. I have spoken with him about the dark doings under your roof. He knows the evil started when the demon arrived."

"The only dark doings at Ravenskirk are in your mind. Mayhap 'tis time for you to seek shelter with your cousin's family."

He shook his head. "The bishop will see the lands cleansed. I have a message for you, from the bishop. Turn the faerie over for questioning within a se'nnight or—"

"Who is this faerie you speak of?"

The man's face turned crimson. "The evil one. Charlotte Merriweather. You have seen how she behaves, the strange things she says. Her beauty is unnatural. A woman so comely must be in league with the devil or a faerie. To save her soul she must be burnt. Before she corrupts all the men at Ravenskirk."

"I am most appreciative how you look out for the welfare of those under my care, Timothy." The man scowled at him, and it gave Henry great pleasure to say, "Though I must refuse your bishop. Mistress Merriweather is under my protection. She is not evil. She is not a devil or a faerie or a demon. She is merely a woman. And I will not give her to you. For I know what kind of *questioning* takes place under the bishop's care."

Timothy scowled and puffed up. "You will regret this. If you do not turn her over, he will confiscate all that you own. You would not want that to happen, not after your family worked so hard to regain what was lost. You will bring shame upon your brothers." Timothy stomped out of the room, slamming the door.

That would teach Henry to ever allow the bishop to visit Ravenskirk again. His timid little priest, Father Riley, would be happy the man was gone.

Henry turned to Royce, who rested his hand on the hilt of his sword.

"What think you?"

"You should've run him through." Royce paced the room, thinking. Henry had known him since they were boys. They fostered together, fought together, and became friends. He respected his captain's judgment.

Finally he stopped pacing and looked at Henry. "There is only one solution." He grinned, and Henry knew he was not going to like what was said next.

"Now hear me out, Henry. You must marry Mistress Merriweather. The bishop would not come for your wife. He would not dare to anger the Thornton brothers. Not with all your gold and powerful armies. The king would get involved, and the bishop would have to explain his actions. Nay, to save her and your lands, you must marry the wench. Let the bishop find someone else to steal from."

"Marry her? You of all people know I cannot."

His captain quirked a brow. "The vow is not binding. It was made when you were in your cups. Talk to the priest. You know there is no other way."

"You know the hatred my parents felt for each other. You, above all, know how difficult they made life for one another. I do not desire such a union."

"Not all marriages are so full of misery. Many husbands

and wives come to care for one another. I have seen you with children, Henry. You like children. Don't you want your own? Heirs?"

"My brothers will have children. I could already have bastards. Mayhap dozens of them all over the country."

His captain threw back his head and laughed. "You have no bastards. If you did, the women would come for you. You are one of the most eligible nobles in the realm. You and your brothers. They would not hesitate to claim what they thought was rightfully theirs." Royce walked over and put a hand on Henry's arm.

"'Tis time to grow up. Let go of childish beliefs."

"My brothers aren't married. None of us desire to trap ourselves in such unions." He looked at the man, hoping for another choice. "Is there no other way? Tell me you can find another way out of this."

Royce shook his head. "I am sorry, Henry. There is no other way. You must marry her and do it now. The bishop will not hesitate to move against you. We both know he will not give you the full se'nnight."

Henry threw his cup against the wall, the pottery shattering. Instead of replying, his captain left the room, shutting the door behind him.

He liked Charlotte. Cared for her a great deal. But he had no desire to marry. She was enchanting, yet if they married she would change. Grow to hate him, as he would her. He had seen it with many couples. Henry stood staring out the window, unseeing.

As the day turned to night, he let loose a great, weary

sigh and stood up straight. Bloody hell, he was a Thornton and a knight of the realm. Lands, title, gold, his people, and Charlotte. All were under his protection. To save her, he would do what needs be done.

Chapter Twenty-Two

Henry spent a restless night. No matter what he thought of, it all led back to him protecting her with his name. What would she say when he told her the news? Not ready to tell her, he spent the morning in the lists working his way through the men.

Sweat ran down his face. Still he was in a foul temper. There was trouble brewing with Lord Hallsey, they had not found her sisters, the fever sickness was coming closer to Ravenskirk, and he was running out of time. Henry cursed viciously. No more wasting time. He saw Addie with a basket over her arm. The child followed Charlotte around night and day.

"Have you seen Mistress Merriweather?"

She skipped along through the great hall. "Follow me. She's in the garden. We're planting flowers."

"I didn't know you could eat flowers. Don't vegetables belong in a garden?"

"You're so silly. You always need a little bit of something

pleasing, that's what my lady says."

He smiled. Charlotte had won over the people in the time she'd been at Ravenskirk. They all treated her as the lady of the castle. He sent up a prayer. *Please don't let me have the kind of marriage my parents had.* Was it possible? He'd seen so many marriages where the man a woman barely tolerated each other. Henry had always thought he would have someone he could talk with. Someone intelligent. A woman who cared about his lands as much as he. Charlotte was all those things. Mayhap their union would not turn bitter.

"Mistress Merriweather. I hear tell every garden needs flowers."

She was kneeling in the dirt. Henry offered a hand to help her up. She brushed the dirt off her skirts as she stood, and he was struck again by her beauty. It would not be so unpleasant to wake up next to her every day. And if they had children? They would be the most beautiful children in all the realm.

She put a hand up over her eyes to shade them from the sun. Then, seeing his face, she stiffened.

"Addie, thank you for your help today. I'm going to rest and talk with Lord Ravenskirk. Go to the kitchens and tell the cook to give you one of the small cakes we made."

The little girl giggled, picked up the basket full of green things, and ran toward the kitchens.

"From the look on your face, I'm afraid you're going to tell me something I don't want to hear." Her hands were clenched in her lap. "News about my sisters?"

He sat next to her. A short stone wall enclosed the garden. There was a bench in each corner. 'Twas a most pleasant place.

The sun turned her hair gold. Henry resisted the urge to twist a lock around his fingers. "There is no news as of yet about your sisters. My brothers are sending messengers out across the realm. If they are in England, we will know."

Henry thought of John. His older brother always knew what to say. Could deliver bad news without sounding like a dolt. Henry missed him still. Wished he were here now to tell Charlotte what must happen.

"'Tis a grave matter indeed. Know I have spent much time thinking on another way, but there is none."

She looked up at him, a smudge of dirt on her nose. Henry reached out with his thumb and wiped it off. His hand hovered in front of her face. He wanted to stroke her cheek, run his finger over her lips. Truth be told, he wanted to kiss her. But now was not the time. He pulled back and the spell was broken.

"Timothy is cousin to a powerful bishop. The corrupt man has coveted my land, my brothers' land, and our gold ever since we each received our castle from our father. He is ever watchful. Looking for reason to confiscate all. And now I fear he has one."

Her eyes widened. Today, next to the growing things in the garden, they looked the gray of the water around the castle after a summer rainstorm. She was kind and good. She would understand.

"What's happened? That little weasel is nothing more

than a troublemaker. I knew from the moment I laid eyes on him. And he obviously hates women."

"Aye. He believes all women to be evil." Henry looked up to see a small boy coming toward them, and was grateful for the distraction. "Would you care for a glass of wine? I fear you will need it by the time our speech is done."

Her sun-kissed skin paled, but she didn't say a word.

"What are the small cakes you spoke of to Addie?"

She smiled at the boy and accepted the wine. "I call them cupcakes. I hope you don't mind we used the expensive flour to make them. And some of the sugar." She blushed and said, "And some of your spices. I'm afraid the small cakes cost a great deal of money. But you can taste for yourself—here comes Addie."

The little girl ran toward them with a basket over her arm.

Henry ruffled the boy's hair. "A cake for you, then off to do your chores."

The boy let out a whoop and reached for a cake. Addie smacked his hand, making Henry bite his cheek to keep from laughing at the boy's expression.

She pulled back the cloth covering the basket. "You may choose one."

"Thank ye, Addie." The boy took a bite and groaned. "I will do your chores for a fortnight for another."

She giggled and, with a look at Charlotte, handed the boy another cake. Then she turned to Henry. "Mrs. Benton says to bring you the small cakes before we eat them all." With a frown, she put her hands on her little hips. "I would never eat all the cakes, not like the boys. They're always eating."

Charlotte covered her mouth but couldn't hold in her laughter. Hearing her made him laugh as well.

"Thank you for bringing them. I was just telling Lord Ravenskirk about them."

Addie held out a small, round cake. He took a bite—truth be told, a rather large bite. Right. Half the bloody cake went in his mouth. He chewed. Sweetness filled his mouth. He looked up to find them grinning.

Henry wiped his mouth and looked at Charlotte. "Spend as much as you desire to make more of these cakes. Delicious."

He had wasted enough time. Henry ate one more cake, drained the wine, and faced her. "Timothy swears you are a faerie. Or perhaps a demon or the devil incarnate."

She started to laugh, then stopped upon seeing his expression. Did he look so fearsome?

"Is that as bad as being considered a witch?"

He nodded. "'Tis a grave matter, Charlotte." He watched her jump.

"You've never called me by my name before. This must be serious."

"Timothy met with the bishop and swore before him that you are all of these things. I am commanded to turn you over for questioning within the se'nnight."

"Where do I have to go? What happens when he questions me?"

Henry shook his head. "The kind of 'questioning' the bishop performs ends up with you likely tortured and then dead."

"Hells bells. I'd forgotten those kinds of things still happen." Her voice trembled as she said, "When are you planning to send me to the bishop?"

Odd. What did she mean, *these kinds of things still happen*? There was something strange about Charlotte he could not put his finger on. But it would have to wait. They had more important matters to discuss.

"Nay, Charlotte. I would never turn you over to that man. He is corrupt and would not hesitate to use you for his own gains. But I fear once I tell you the only way to save you, you may wish I had turned you over."

Chapter Twenty-Three

Henry thought Charlotte looked as he felt. She swallowed and looked in her cup as if it held the answers to the very heavens above. "I think I'm going to need more wine to hear any more." Henry called one of the servants over and sent them to fetch more wine. They sat in silence waiting. Neither wanting to continue their speech.

The man came back and left the jug of wine. Henry poured another glass for her. She drank half of it and set the goblet down beside her on the bench. He watched as she sat up tall, looking as regal as any queen.

"Whatever it is, I'm ready. Tell me."

"If I refuse to turn you over, I forfeit everything I own. My land, my gold, Ravenskirk. And then he will send soldiers to take you by force. The man is cruel. You would suffer horribly. Those under my protection would no longer be safe. They too would suffer. The only way to save you and my people...is for us to marry."

She blinked at him. Her mouth opened and closed, and

he watched as her skin turned from a lovely rosy color to the color of the first winter snow. With a shaking hand, she drained the rest of the wine, poured another goblet, drank it down, and poured yet another.

"I'm sure I heard you correctly, but did you say we have to get married? As in 'I do,' rings, cake, and a big white dress?"

"We shall have the small cakes you make after the ceremony and the feast. You may wear whatever dress you like. You will have one made."

She held up a hand. "Stop. I was making a jest. But I see I should not have. I can't marry you."

"Are you betrothed?"

"No. I'm not engaged and I'm not married. But we can't marry. We don't even really know each other."

"Many marriages are arranged. The first time a man sees his new wife may be at the ceremony." He winced. "My own parents did not know each other. Truth be told, they could not stand to be in the same room together. I care for you and hope that in time you would come to care for me."

She looked like she was ready to bolt or faint, so Henry took her arm and pulled her close. "A walk on the battlements always does me good."

When they reached the top of the battlements and started pacing, Henry spoke again.

"Is there anyone who can aid you? Any other family? I could send you to them wherever you come from. The bishop's reach would not extend to another country."

She shook her head. "No, there is no one and it is too

far."

His pride suffered as he saw how desolate she looked.

"If we can't find Lucy or Melinda, I am all alone," she whispered.

"You will never be alone with me by your side. I swear it."

"This is not what I expected." She tripped, and he caught her arm. Henry thought she looked like a frightened deer.

"As Lady Ravenskirk you will be safe. The bishop will not risk the wrath of my brothers by taking my lady wife. And the king would involve himself in the affair. We would declare war, my brothers would send armies and gold, but I have seen too much bloodshed and would prefer not to send men to their deaths when we can prevent it." He took her hand. "I do not wish to marry either."

Had he imagined it, or did she flinch? He looked at her like she was a mystery he couldn't quite work out.

She didn't speak, but continued to walk. Henry let her think, walking back and forth next to her, watching the fast flutter at her neck. As close as he stood, he thought he could hear her heart beating as fast as a galloping horse. He walked until his feet started to ache. The sun was low in the sky by the time she sat down on a low bench and let out a great sigh.

"I can think of no other way around this. But isn't there someone you care for? Are you betrothed?"

Henry shook his head. "Nay. I am not promised. There is no one. I vowed never to marry." He shook his head. "The fates are laughing at me. One should never make a vow about marriage or matters of the heart."

"Oh, Henry. I am so very sorry. I only wanted to find my sisters. You probably wish you'd never rescued me off that beach. You've been so kind, shown me hospitality, and this is how you are repaid. I will run away."

"The bishop's men would find you. He knows I would come for you. I will not allow you to be harmed. As my wife, you will have the protection of my name. As Charlotte Thornton, Lady Ravenskirk, no one will dare speak ill of you. No harm will come to you. The bishop will go away and try to steal from someone else, and I will try my best not to kill Timothy for what he has done. Though I will banish him forevermore from Ravenskirk."

He took her hands in his. "As my wife, you also have the protection of my brothers. They will stand with me if anyone tries to harm you. What say you, Charlotte Merriweather? Will you consent to marry me?"

She shook her head. "Wait. Did you say your name is Henry *Thornton*? I don't know why I never asked. I knew you were Lord Ravenskirk, but for some reason I never thought to ask your last name."

She was looking at him as if a question had been answered, and he couldn't tell if the look was one of fear or joy.

"Is aught amiss?"

Charlotte hesitated, as if she was going to tell him something, and Henry knew once again she was keeping secrets. He only hoped she wasn't in league with Lord Hallsey. For soon he would be tied to her forever.

"No, nothing's wrong. I just didn't know your last name."
She started for the door that would lead them back inside
the castle, turned, and said, "All the musicians that have
played here, I've never heard a piper. Does one usually play
for you?"

'Twas a strange question. Henry thought about it. "Nay.
One passed through a year or so ago. My brother John had a
piper, and so does my eldest brother, Edward. John loved
the music; said 'twas his favorite. He died years ago."

"I'm sorry. I know what it is to lose those you hold dear."
He felt the trembling, yet she did not weep.

She looked sad. "I had always hoped if I ever did find the
right guy, we would marry for love. I cannot let you do this."

With the lightest touch, she stopped him in the
courtyard. "Turn me over. I'll find a way out of this mess.
You've done more than enough to help me."

"You would be tortured. Have you ever seen the inside of
a dungeon?"

At the shake of her head, he nodded. "I thought not. Nay,
Charlotte. 'Tis my knightly duty to aid you, and I will marry
you to save you from the bishop. My name and my family
will protect you." He dropped to one knee.

"I ask you once more, will you marry me?"

Her eyes full of tears, she favored him with a small smile.
"I will. I can never thank you enough for saving me."

He nodded stiffly. They walked into the great hall to eat
supper. As a member of a most powerful family, Henry
could arrange a hasty ceremony. The bishop would be full of
fury when he found out Charlotte was no longer within his

reach—and even angrier to know Thornton lands and gold had escaped his greedy grasp once again.

Chapter Twenty-Four

Marriage. To a medieval noble. Sure, she had a huge crush on Henry. Who wouldn't? And yes, she really liked him a lot. But love? It took time to fall in love. To know without a doubt this was the person you could picture yourself growing old with. Charlotte sat back on her heels in the garden and wiped a dirty hand across her brow.

"Are you ill, mistress?" Addie peered up at her. "You have a strange look upon your face."

"I'm not ill. Just thinking."

The girl smiled. "You're going to be Lady Ravenskirk. You'll be very rich, and Lord Ravenskirk is most handsome."

"And you will still help me in the gardens."

The horrified look on Addie's face made Charlotte laugh.

"Nay, you cannot work in the gardens. Fine noble ladies do not do such things."

"I think fine noble ladies do as they wish. And I wish to work in the garden."

The girl looked scandalized as she pondered what

Charlotte said. Finally, she wrinkled her nose and said, "'Tis rather nice to plant and watch things grow. I like the flowers best. I don't care for how dirt smells."

"It is a nice feeling." Charlotte looked at the girl. "I rather like the smell of the earth. Reminds me we're all here for such a short time. Now take the basket of herbs into the kitchens."

As the child scampered away, Charlotte sat back against the cool stone wall, tilting her face up to the sun.

She must've fallen asleep. When she woke, her wrist was sore from sitting on it. Charlotte yawned. It felt good to stretch. What she wouldn't give for a yoga class right now. Many times she'd been tempted to practice, but fear of being branded a witch kept her from it. There was always someone around. Even in the privacy of her chamber she was worried Addie or someone else would walk in.

A sound made her look up. Where was it coming from? In the time she'd been at the castle, she'd come to recognize the various sounds. Swords clanging, animals, people coming and going, the sound of the blacksmith, and other everyday noises.

But this...something was out of place. She needed a better vantage point. The battlements would be perfect.

Up top, she slowly walked around until she came to the far northern corner. This section was guarded by the three men she used to see with Timothy. Charlotte peered into the woods when she heard the sound again. It seemed to come when the man on duty was at the opposite end of the battlements.

She caught a flash of green, not leaves or the wind blowing the trees. It was as if someone were moving. Trying not to be seen. She blinked and it was gone. Charlotte was trying to decide if her eyes were playing tricks on her when Chester appeared. He popped up throughout the day whenever Henry wasn't with her.

"Lady?"

"I thought I saw someone moving in the woods. Wearing a green tunic. When I looked again, they were gone."

Chester peered over the wall into the woods. He went stiff, speaking in a quiet voice. "My lady, act as if nothing is amiss. I will find my lord."

She walked beside him. "What's wrong?"

He shook his head. "I am not sure, but we have had much trouble with Lord Hallsey and his men. 'Tis better to send men out to scout the area."

He spoke to the sentry on duty while she tried to nonchalantly walk along the battlements, stopping here and there to look out over the walls into the water. With the breeze making ripples on the surface, she couldn't see her reflection today. Living in a castle in the middle of the water felt like being on your own private island. This was now her home, or would be soon.

Married. After watching her friends graduate college and marry, seeing her sisters' friends marry and start having babies, after so many failed relationships, she'd given up. Maybe all those boyfriends were practice for Henry. He was the real deal, and she hoped as they kept getting to know each other, he would love her.

Ever since the castle inhabitants found out she was going to marry Henry, they'd quit calling her mistress and started calling her lady. They'd all accepted her without question. And for that she was grateful. The lady of the castle. Charlotte still couldn't wrap her head around the idea.

What a huge difference from her own time. In the future, the church had no such power. If someone threatened her, she would've simply gone to the authorities. But here, things were very different. She knew how much the people relied on him. Had heard stories of other lords and how awful they could be. Henry was an anomaly in how much he cared about the welfare of his people.

Charlotte had agreed to marry him because she could see no other way. Being tortured and killed was certainly not on her list of desirable things to do, and she'd feel responsible if Henry lost everything. So she agreed. In time, she'd hoped they'd continue their relationship, but she'd thought it would be years, not days before the subject of marriage came up.

She was in her chamber, washing off a day's worth of dirt, when there was a knock at the door. Henry strode in, and she was struck again by how handsome he was.

"I hope I didn't cause you to send men out for nothing.

My eyes were probably playing tricks on me."

"'Twas a scout. One of Hallsey's men." He led her over to the window and pointed. "His lands are to the north. He would like nothing more than to take Ravenskirk and control access to all the land to the south."

"Are we in danger?"

"I think not. After we killed the men responsible for burning the village, he will be loath to lose more. Though I have doubled the guard to be safe. Edward would strike. My brother stabs first and questions later."

"How many brothers do you have again?"

"Five. Edward is the eldest. And there was John. Then me, Robert, and Christian. Christian is the youngest at a score and two."

"You're how old?"

"I am a score and seven."

"You must be awfully good at being a knight to have done so well for yourself at such a young age. I'm still trying to figure out what I want to be when I grow up." She laughed. "I guess now I will be Lady Ravenskirk."

Charlotte put a hand to her throat. "I'm still trying to get used to the idea, so I go around saying 'Lady Ravenskirk' all day. I think everyone believes I'm daft."

Henry chuckled. "They already think of you as my lady. Many of them have told me I should have married you the day I found you." They sat down in the window seat and he stroked her cheek.

"I am truly the luckiest man in the realm. You are kind and beautiful. Intelligent and strong. Any man would be lucky to have you for a wife." He looked into her eyes, and Charlotte wanted to lose herself in him.

His voice came out as a whisper. "I have come to care for you a great deal. I hope in time you will feel the same. Mayhap one day, we will love each other." He leaned forward and gently kissed her. He paused for a moment, his lips an inch from hers, and Charlotte felt the tension between them filling the room. It seemed to stretch out and out until finally it snapped.

Henry pulled her to him and kissed her again. The kiss was not gentle. It was the kiss of a man who cared for his woman. She lost herself to the feelings. The sensation traveled from her head all the way down to her toes, as they tingled. When he sat back, she put her fingers to her lips. They felt bruised and swollen, and she thought she must have a goofy smile on her face. He smiled at her in the way that men seemed to do when they were particularly happy with themselves.

"I will be counting the minutes until I see you in the hall for dinner."

Oh my. She was in deep trouble. He was kind, responsible, and thoughtful. Not to mention charming, handsome, rich, and a great kisser. Yes indeed, she was in trouble.

Charlotte could almost hear Aunt Pittypat from the great beyond laughing hysterically. Whenever she complained she couldn't find a good boyfriend, her aunt always said not to worry. For when she finally found the man meant for her, she would fall, and fall hard.

Aunt Pittypat was always right.

Chapter Twenty-Five

"You own all this?" Charlotte couldn't believe it. "Are you richer than the King of England?"

He laughed. "Nay. My brother Edward is, though."

She sat across from him. All morning she'd been distracted and hadn't accomplished anything. Charlotte joined Henry in the solar for a few moments of quiet.

"I don't have much to offer. This is all I own." She untied the scarf and dumped the coins and gems on a small table.

"You have much to offer. I care not for gold and gems." He looked through her offering. It was odd to see the old coins back in the time they belonged.

"There is a great deal here."

She snorted. "Not compared to you. I would like to add it to the household for whatever is needed."

"Keep it for yourself to use as you see fit." Henry rubbed the material of the scarf between his fingers. "Such fine workmanship. The craftsmen in your lands are skilled."

For machines, she thought. "Thank you."

"Charlotte?"

The look on his face made her tense. "I'm going out for a walk. It's a beautiful day."

"Wait." He ran a hand through his hair and stretched out in the chair, hands folded across his stomach. The somber look made her even more nervous.

"What is it?"

"Would you prefer to live elsewhere? I will see you settled in your own estate. With men to guard you and ladies of your choosing. You need not remain with me."

She blinked. Hurt sliced through her heart, so sharp that for a minute she thought she was having a heart attack. All the emotion she'd felt since Lucy went missing, then Melinda, bubbled up. The fear when that man tried to kill her, and the sensations of traveling through time. Her own insecurities about men. It was too much.

Charlotte stood, one hand on her hip, one finger pointed at Henry.

"I understand you're sacrificing a great deal by marrying me. If you don't want me around, just say so. Quit being so damned charming and solicitous." Her finger trembled, but her voice rang out across the room as the fury built to hurricane status inside her.

"Charlotte, perchance you misunderstand me."

She narrowed her eyes at him. Henry, sensing the change in mood, jumped up from his chair and stood in front of the windows, hands out in front of him. Too late; she was in a state, as her sisters used to say. He better run.

"I guess I should be grateful you're not packing me off to

a convent. Will this estate be anywhere near Ravenskirk? You'll come visit me once or twice a year so we can have an heir to continue your name? I will not be locked away to sit and wait for the mighty lord to visit me." Charlotte poked him in the chest.

"We can speak reasonably. You are vexed."

"No you didn't. Did you just tell me to calm down? You have a hell of a nerve, Mr. Prince Charming. I've heard all about you. The women here have filled my ears with tales of your conquests. You must have women in every village in the entire country, and probably France and Scotland too! I thought you were charming, but you're nothing more than a womanizing pig! Take your offer of an estate and go to hell. I'd rather be drawn and quartered and my head used as a fricking bowling ball than marry an ass like you!"

She stomped out of the room, slamming the door.

Royce stuck his head in, grinning. "The lady sounds most displeased."

Henry was bewildered. "What did I do? I offered Charlotte her own estate where she could live in peace if she so desired."

"You told her to go?"

He ran his hands through his hair. "I thought she might

not want to remain here with me." He threw back the contents of his mug. "She has a fearsome temper."

"She thinks you do not want her as your wife. That you are marrying her to save her and your own sorry self. Women want to be wooed."

"I'm giving her the protection of my name. My body. She will want for nothing." Henry stalked back and forth across the solar. He needed his sword. "To the lists."

"The men have made themselves scarce. They heard Mistress Charlotte bellowing, and you will not see them until supper."

He cursed. "She knows I am not a prince. Why did she call me one?" He scratched his head. "And I know what a pig is, but what is 'womanizing'?"

"From her speech, 'tis a man who enjoys the favors of many women while remaining true to none."

"Bloody hell. I have not shown another favor since I rescued Charlotte. I cannot change what happened in the past. How can she be angry with me?"

His childhood friend snorted. "Women. Who knows why they do the things they do. But Henry, you marry her in three days. Make it right or lose everything. Again."

"And what is a bowling ball?" All the time Charlotte had been here he'd never seen her thunder and bellow as she did today. He must send her away. He could not bear her to scream at him every day the way his parents treated one another. He would marry her as 'twas his knightly duty, but he would not remain by her side. All women were the same: marry them and any affection turned to hatred. Lasting until their dying breath.

Chapter Twenty-Six

Three days passed in a blur. Was it really her wedding day? How did you marry someone you weren't even speaking to?

Charlotte thought Henry cared for her. She knew he liked her. Hadn't they moved beyond like to something deeper? In time, she would call it love. Grumpy, she drank another cup of wine.

The next thing she knew, Charlotte found herself standing outside, the sun shining down on her, in front of the chapel. Father Riley beamed at her then ducked his head. The man was shy and stumbled over his words. She didn't know why he was nervous; he wasn't the one getting married to someone who planned to ship him off to another house for the foreseeable future.

A shadow fell across the ground in front of her. Charlotte looked up as the raven cawed, circling above her head. The bird landed on top of the chapel as if watching the proceedings.

It wasn't too late to stop this farce. She would ask him for a horse and a guide to Falconburg or Blackford. Surely they wouldn't turn her over to the bishop. *He'll lose everything. The people will suffer. Are you willing to take the responsibility?*

The priest cleared his throat, and she realized she was scowling at him. Now if she told Henry she was from the future, he might lock her up. She'd gotten by so far without having to tell him. Based on everything she'd seen, medieval England was crazy superstitious. While he seemed reasonable and open to new ideas, she kept thinking what she would do if someone told her they were from the past or from the future.

Charlotte snorted, and Henry raised a brow. She shook her head. Jerk.

She'd call the authorities and have them locked up without a second glance. And so she would keep her secret, hoping the powers that be would understand. Didn't all couples come to a marriage with at least some kind of secret between them?

Henry shifted, and she hoped he was as miserable as she. And wasn't that mean and snippy? He wasn't cruel, just damaged. Shaped and forged by his past. In his case, his parents' relationship. In hers? She quit believing in love after a disastrous high school relationship.

First love. Spencer Todd had been her world. Smart, athletic, nice to everyone. Or so she thought. At the time she was going through a chunky phase, and was shocked when he'd expressed interest. They dated most of sophomore year. He was two years older than her. He invited her to prom. Excited, she and Aunt Pittypat spent the day getting ready. She waited and waited. He never showed up. Never answered his phone or texts. It was all over social media. He'd taken the stuck-up skinny cheerleader. Said he'd never liked a fatty like her. Only dated her to see if she'd put out. After that, Charlotte dated but never gave her heart away again.

Or so she thought. Henry had stolen a chunk when she wasn't looking. Father Riley stuttered on, and Charlotte decided she was done. The marriage would proceed to save his people and her own skin. She would use his money, influence, and men to find her sisters, and she would live wherever he sent her. It wasn't as if she could go home. She was stuck in 1330 medieval England, and being married to a powerful noble was the best she could hope for. They would be civil to one another, but she'd be damned if she'd provide him an heir. He could knock up some village girl for all she cared.

Charlotte sniffed. No, she would not cry. Instead she bit the inside of her cheek until she tasted blood. The wind blew the ribbons holding her hair back. They were dark blue to match her dress. That morning she'd been presented with the most amazing dress. It was dark blue with embroidery all over the neckline sleeves and hem. It even had pockets, as Henry had seen them in her dress and knew how fond she was of them. A few of the women had helped her get ready and put her hair up. It was in a mass of curls, and she'd never felt so beautiful in all her life. Pretty and empty inside.

The small things in life. Like someone noticing something you liked and doing it for you without being asked. Pain shot down her arm and side. Why didn't he care for her the way she cared for him? His actions told her he cared, but after what he said?

It was as if she was having an out-of-body experience. Charlotte knew she was standing in front of the chapel, reciting vows, and yet it didn't seem as if she were truly present.

She heard something about a ring, felt something heavy and cool slide over her fourth finger. A wide gold band with a large dark amethyst shone in the sunlight.

Just great. She didn't have a ring for him. Before he told her he was sending her away, she'd made a mental note to have one made, but then everything blew apart. Just as she was about to have a major meltdown from the emotions of the past few days, she felt a tug on her dress. It was Addie.

"My lady. Chester and I took the coins and the sapphire from your bag and had a ring made," the little girl whispered as she pressed a wide gold band carved with ravens and set with a beautiful sapphire into her hand.

Charlotte looked at her blankly.

"Don't you remember, lady? We did ask your permission."

Heck, all she remembered from the past few days was being furious all the time. This wasn't the time or place to show her butt, as her aunt would have said.

"Thank you," she whispered as she accepted the ring.

Addie had come from a noble family to serve as a lady's

maid at the castle, but for some reason she and Addie had never talked about her parents. Charlotte felt bad and made a note to rectify the situation as soon as things calmed down. Would the girl want to go with her to her new home, wherever it was?

She exhaled and slid the ring on Henry's finger. It fit perfectly. Too bad they no longer fit together.

Chapter Twenty-Seven

Henry softly knocked at the door to his own chamber. No, 'twas their chamber now. He ducked as he entered in case she threw something at him. After she raged at him, she had refused to speak to him. Not a word from then until the wedding this afternoon. And then she only answered the vows. During supper she sat quietly, speaking to others when asked a question but otherwise ignoring him.

He'd tried several times to engage her in speech, but she rebuffed his attempts.

The women led her to their chamber to make her ready for the wedding night. She threw a pitcher at him when he entered. Told him hell would freeze over before he touched her. Some of her curses...he'd never heard the like, but understood the meaning.

Finally he'd gone across the hall to her room and slept there. Hours later he'd woken. He was an arse. Of course she was angry. She thought he did not want her. He did.

In trying to offer her a way to live apart if she did not

want him, he had caused her great offense. He truly cared for her. In her place, he too would be angry. From the moment he'd met her, she had been kind and caring. She was not his mother. He was not his father. Together they were well matched. He would make her understand his meaning.

'Twas early, still dark outside, when he knocked on the door.

"Charlotte. 'Tis time to talk. You cannot remain angry with me the rest of your life."

"Of course I can."

"Will you hear me out?"

"Whatever."

He wasn't sure what *whatever* meant, but he was a warrior. Henry took a breath.

"I was an arse."

She snorted.

"I let my parents' life influence me. I do not want to be apart from you. I only offered you the estate so you would not feel you had to stay at Ravenskirk with me the rest of your life if you did not desire to."

The light from the fire showed her curves through her chemise. She was beautiful and strong. He wanted her by his side. Needed her.

"Please accept my apology. I care for you a great deal. I believe in time we will grow to love one another. Will you forgive me?"

A tear fell, and Henry wanted to curse. Never again would he be the cause of her tears.

"When you offered me the estate, I thought you didn't want me around. And after all the stories I heard about your past, I figured you wanted the freedom to be with other women without having me near." She wrapped her arms around herself, and Henry took a step forward. Seeing the look on her face, he stopped.

"I realize your past is simply that. The past. When I was sixteen, someone hurt me very badly." She sighed. "I need to work through my own issues. Given we had to marry, well, I didn't know how you felt about me." Her voice wavered.

Henry took her in his arms, stroking her hair. "I have been miserable without you by my side. Stay with me. I will do everything in my power to make amends. I care for you a great deal. I know in time I will love you."

"In time, I think I will love you too. I'm sorry too. I said some hateful things. Forgive me for being such a witch?"

Then she let out a shaky laugh. "I don't mean a real witch. A witch is someone who isn't very nice where I come from."

"I would forgive you anything, Charlotte."

Charlotte woke in the morning to find Henry gone. Last night she didn't think she'd eaten more than a few bites during supper. But she'd had way too much to drink. The women had finished undressing her, making all kinds of lewd suggestions as to how she should spend her wedding night. She kept thinking he could have their marriage annulled whenever he got sick of her.

The women left tittering and calling out a few more suggestions. They'd left a plate with some fruit, cheese, and bread, along with plenty of wine.

She sat in front of a low fire staring into the flames. A quiet knock sounded and Henry came into the room. It was a relief he wanted to talk. Stubborn as a mule, her sisters liked to say. At least she'd listened without throwing anything. She was still embarrassed for totally going ballistic and throwing the pitcher at him. Never in her whole life had she behaved in such a way. Aunt Pittypat would have been horrified.

They'd spend the remainder of the night sleeping next to each other. When she woke, she felt as if she hadn't slept at all. Too much emotional upheaval over the past few days and the added energy drain from their talk last night.

The door opened as she dropped the cloth in the basin and reached for her chemise. Henry gasped. "You have writing on your body." He walked over to her. "May I?"

Charlotte held the chemise in front of her, baring her side. "They're called tattoos."

He knelt, tracing the words with a finger, raising goosebumps on her flesh. What would it be like to feel his touch over the rest of her body?

"'The soul is here for its own joy.'" Henry looked up at her, his breath warm against her skin as he spoke. "'Tis a beautiful saying."

On his knees, he leaned closer, his hair tickling her flesh.

"Om. What is Om?" Henry peered up at her. "The sound of the universe smiling."

He leaned back on his heels, looking at her, then it was as if he suddenly realized she was standing there naked before him, except for the chemise covering the important bits.

Henry stumbled to his feet and turned around. "My apologies."

She pulled the chemise over her head, then the dress. "I'm afraid I can't do the rest by myself. I'll call for Addie."

"I will aid you." Henry fastened up the dress. It was oddly intimate, him helping her dress. Every day now it would be this way. She was aware of the tiniest movement, his fingers tying laces, his breath on her skin, and the smell of him. Charlotte leaned into him. There was a charge in the air. He gave her a look so full of heat she felt like she was the only woman in the entire world.

"You are the kind of woman men go to war for." He captured her mouth, and Charlotte kissed him back like a drowning woman given oxygen. They were perfect together.

Henry dispatched a messenger to the bishop to inform

him of the good news. "Make haste, man. The bishop will surely want to send his blessing to the new lady of Ravenskirk."

He smirked as the messenger rode out. And continued to smirk as the man rode across the bridge and out of sight.

The swordsmith hastily jumped up. "My lord, how may I be of service?"

"I would like to give my lady two daggers as a wedding gift." Henry opened the pouch at his waist, pulling out two stones, which he handed to the man. Fulbert was a bear of a man and kin to his brother Edward's blacksmith.

Fulbert examined the stones. "The amethyst and sapphire are a good size for the hilts. Was there anything in particular you wanted on the hilt and blade?"

"Flowers and vines carved on the hilt around the stone. On the blade with the amethyst, the word *Om* seven times and then the words *The sound of the universe smiling.*"

The man looked dubious but nodded. "And the sapphire?"

"The same carvings and the words *The soul is here for its own joy.*"

Fulbert grunted. "'Tis a lovely saying." The man scratched his beard. "Boots."

"Boots?"

"Aye. The lady can keep her daggers in the boots. Much easier than reaching through her skirts or in a belt at her waist."

Henry nodded. He would have a new pair of boots made for her. He clapped the man on the back. "I thank ye."

It was time Henry took Charlotte to Falconburg and then on to Blackford. The sickness was abating, and it would soon be safe to travel. If they found no answers, he would take her to each of his brothers' castles. He wanted them to meet his new wife. And to aid her in finding her sisters. Charlotte would be pleased. Henry was happier than he had been in a long time. As he strode across the courtyard, his captain ran up to him. The look on his face wiped away Henry's high spirits.

"We are under siege."

"Bloody hell. Get everyone inside. Dismantle the bridge and close the gates."

"'Tis already underway."

Where was Charlotte? He had to find her. Ensure her safety. She liked to leave the castle and forage for wildflowers. As if in answer to his unasked question, Royce placed a hand on Henry's shoulder.

"Do not fear; your lady is safe. She is in the kitchen going over the contents of the larder and storerooms with Mrs. Benton."

"How did this happen with no warning? Who was on duty?"

"The three men watching the north and west should have sounded the alarm. They are now missing. In league with Timothy."

Henry swore.

Chapter Twenty-Eight

The castle was under siege. Henry assured her this had never happened before. They would be trapped on what amounted to an island. Charlotte forced herself to stop, stand still, and practice breathing. There wasn't time for a panic attack. Wasn't time to fall to pieces. She must do whatever she could to help. Not only because anyone would, but because she was now the lady of the castle and was expected to do so.

She'd been outside the castle walls looking at land to plan an orchard and another garden when Liam threw her on the back of a horse and rode like hell for the castle.

That was when she spotted the army of men coming out of the woods. It looked like rush hour in the Tokyo subway, or an anthill knocked over. She'd never dreamt her heart could beat so fast or so loud. Charlotte was wild with fear, panting for breath and seeing spots by the time they thundered across the bridge.

"Thank goodness the villagers are already here." She

tugged on Liam's tunic. "What about the people outside the walls?"

"They are here, lady. And look, the rest come."

She watched men, women, and children running for the safety of the castle. No sooner had the people crossed the bridge than men set to work dismantling the thing. Would they get it done before their attackers reached them?

"Come inside the castle, lady."

"No, Liam. I want to see. When the portcullis slams shut, I'll go in."

He looked dubious, but turned to help the other garrison knights.

"Chester, I don't see one of those big siege towers. That's good, right?"

"The land is too uneven for such a tower. They will have the trebuchet."

She gulped. It felt like she was in the middle of a movie. Except this was all too real. And now, along with Henry, she was responsible for the life of every person within the walls. If the village hadn't been burnt to the ground, how many would still be out there? The castle was filled to capacity. Would they have enough food? Hadn't she read somewhere that sieges could last years? Thank goodness they had the two wells within the castle walls so there would be clean drinking water.

The bridge dismantled, the gate slammed down just in time. There were so many men out there. Charlotte was totally out of her depth.

"Open the damn gates, Henry. By rights, Ravenskirk belongs to me. Your father stole it and I will take it back."

Henry stood on the battlements looking down on his enemy. "Fight me. The winner takes Ravenskirk."

"You cheat. In every tourney you cheated. I am the better warrior. I have no need to fight you or steal another man's wife," the man blustered.

"Hallsey, you are weak. I bested you as my sire bested your sire. Leave my lands now and I won't run you through."

"I will starve you out. Then I will kill anyone left alive within the walls and let the crows feast on your bones."

An archer let loose an arrow. Hallsey jumped back, his face mottled with rage. "You will die by my sword, Thornton swine."

Henry threw back his head and laughed. "Come and get me, you great bloody whoreson."

In the kitchens, Charlotte talked with Mrs. Benton as

they went over the foodstuffs.

"Do not fear, lady. We have enough."

"Even with all the extra villagers?"

"We will have enough."

Charlotte thought she looked worried. Didn't it figure? She wanted to stamp her foot and throw a tantrum like the cute little girl who'd lived down the street from her back in Holden Beach.

Every time she thought it would be the right time to finally come clean and tell Henry she was from the future, to tell him the whole story, something happened. When she woke this morning, she'd decided today was the day. Now they'd cleared the air, she didn't want such a big secret between them.

He was her husband even though he'd only married her to save her. She was still his wife, stuck in medieval England. And since her sisters had never come back to the future, Charlotte had to assume she was here permanently. So she would make the best of the situation. And, truth be told, it could be worse. He could've been an old, bald, mean man. Instead she'd gotten the movie star guy. *Let's just hope he lives up to the hype*, said the voice in her head.

Chapter Twenty-Nine

Charlotte wandered aimlessly around Henry's room. Although she had to start thinking of it as their room. All her things had been moved into his chamber. It was large and spacious and smelled of him. The smell of outdoors and sunshine, with a hint of leather.

He pulled her down onto his lap in front of the fire. Out the window, she could see the enemy fires blazing, reflected in the water outside.

"Charlotte Thornton, my lovely wife, I know we will be happy together." He reached into the pouch at his waist and drew something out that sparkled in the candlelight.

"Hold out your arm." It was a bracelet, and as he fastened it around her wrist she felt the room start to spin. She knew the bracelet well. It was an amethyst bracelet set in gold. The gold carved with leaves and flowers. The amethysts rounded and polished, gleaming darkly.

Her vision started to tunnel in as the room receded, everything focusing inward to a tiny pinpoint, until the only thing in her line of sight was the sparkle of gold and amethysts. As if from faraway, Charlotte heard Henry talking to her but couldn't make out the words.

Was it happening? No! She couldn't go back. Not yet. She hadn't found her sisters. Seeing the bracelet on her wrist, the one she'd bought in the shop in London, in 2016 London, made her feel as if her world were about to implode.

There wasn't enough oxygen in the room. Charlotte desperately gulped in air, trying to force breath into her lungs. She wasn't going back to her own time. She was dying. *Please don't let me die. Not yet. I have to find Lucy and Melinda first. I want a chance with Henry. I care deeply for him. Don't let it end before it's begun.*

She came to slowly. Cracking open an eye, she found herself in bed, a cold cloth across her forehead. She felt like she'd been run over by a truck.

"You cried out and fainted." Henry handed her a glass of wine. "Drink. You'll feel better."

"I'm sorry. It was a panic attack. I've gotten them on and off for years. I thought they'd gone away until everything happened with my sisters and I came...here."

"Panic attack?"

"It's hard to explain. It's like you feel as if you're going to die. Like you can't breathe." She drank a little more of the wine and sat up, swaying. He steadied her.

"I won't let you fall."

"When I was eighteen, a boy I liked took me on a boat. It turned out he wasn't very nice, and I spent the night hiding in a tiny closet while he searched for me. I should have known better. There was a terrible storm and it brought back memories of the night my parents died. They were killed in a boating accident when I was little.

"The guy left me on the boat. I was found two days later. He knew I was in the closet, and locked the door so I couldn't get out. My aunt said I didn't speak for a month. And after that, whenever something would upset me or scare me, I would have one of these attacks."

He pulled her into his arms, holding her tight, stroking her hair and mumbling words into her ear. Gently he pulled out each pin, letting her hair tumble free. He combed it with his fingers, listening to her talk. He didn't say a word. He just waited.

"That was almost five years ago. Sometimes it will be months before I have another attack."

"I would never harm you. You do know this, don't you?"

She kissed his cheek. "I know you would not." Should she tell him? It seemed to be the right time, and yet something held her back. So instead she said, "I think it's just the idea of marriage. Finding myself married when I thought I would never get married."

"Mayhap we are suited to each other. Though I think suitors would be lining up to court you."

"I had boyfriends. There were just so many things I wanted to do. I assumed at some point in the future I would get married. I thought had all the time in the world. But as time went by, I realized I wasn't a very good girlfriend. After the two relationship disasters, I never seemed to get it right again. I came to believe I would never marry."

"You know my mother and father hated each other. I did not want to risk the same misery. And marriage is forever. No matter what happens, we must agree to talk to one another. To treat each other as we wish to be treated."

"I wish my sisters could've been here to see me get married." She was wife to a medieval lord. Who would've guessed? Charlotte wondered under what circumstances her sisters might have gotten married. Surely they must be married. Were they happy? Did they love their husbands?

After all she had been through, so many failed relationships, she was afraid of the word *love*. So she would say she cared a great deal for Henry, but she would not utter that four-letter word.

Chapter Thirty

"How fair thee?" Henry sank into the chair in the solar with a weary sigh.

Charlotte passed him a platter of food and a cup of wine to drink.

"What's happening doesn't seem real to me. I've never experienced a siege before, only read about them."

A dark bruise bloomed across his cheek. A villager practicing with a wooden sword had whacked him in the face. The man fell to the ground begging for mercy. Charlotte watched as Henry wiped the blood from his nose and helped the man up. He showed him a few more moves and sent him off to practice. She would have cried like a baby and not have been nearly as nice.

"I've sorted everyone out and assigned jobs. I know we have a large store of food, but do I need to be worried? How long do these things usually last?"

Henry ran his hands through his hair and rolled his shoulders.

"I do not know. The last messenger we sent out was killed before he cleared the woods. I will try again to send word to my brothers. They will send their armies and 'twill all be over soon."

She could tell he was tired by the circles under his eyes. It had been four long days since the siege started. During that time he'd constantly checked on her to make sure she was okay. That she didn't need anything and wasn't afraid. His kind manner and the care he showed to everyone in the castle made her realize she was falling in love with him.

Would they live long enough to enjoy their marriage? Knowing they were surrounded by men who wanted to kill them was turning her into a pessimist.

Charlotte was about to ask him a question when she looked up to see him sound asleep, his chin resting on his chest. She moved the platter away so he wouldn't knock it over and took the cup from his hands, setting it on the table.

For a while she sat and stared at this man who had been kind to her, gone out of his way to help her. Was trying his best to change his views about marriage. She didn't know any men in the future who would have risked so much for her.

Were the men in this time so different, or was it simply a different mentality, the way things were? If it were true, Charlotte thought she would be happy here in the past. She'd come to enjoy the rhythm of the days, the people, and the lack of noise. From cars, planes, and trains, to the overwhelming amount of electronic devices. It was funny; she hadn't noticed all the noise until there wasn't any.

Royce strode into the room. Charlotte put a finger to her lips, rising to greet him. "Let him sleep. He was up all night."

"My lady, that fat bastard has a trebuchet on the way. We heard the men's voices carrying across the water."

"Wait. Those things that throw stuff and smash walls?"

"Indeed. Though it will take time to arrive and be assembled. When Henry wakes, ask him to find me."

"How far is the reach? With the water in between us and them, is it far enough?"

The man shook his head. "Nay. We must send a messenger out. We cannot allow Ravenskirk to fall. Lord Hallsey is a cruel man. He has a dungeon and makes good use of it. He would not hesitate to kill everyone within the walls. Slowly and for his wicked pleasure."

Wasn't that just a delightful thing to hear so early in the day? Charlotte softly closed the door behind her.

Charlotte couldn't believe she was living through a siege. Although she guessed it could be worse. Next year, the war with Scotland would begin, and six years after that the Hundred Years War kicked off. And let's not forget, eighteen years from now, in 1348, the Black Plague would sweep across the lands. Charlotte almost wished she didn't know what was coming.

After dinner, she laid out everyone's work for the next few days. Henry was outside with the men. They were checking the walls for weak spots. With so much happening, time passed quickly, and Charlotte felt like she was the white rabbit, constantly running late. That afternoon she was in the solar taking a few minutes for herself when Henry stumbled in.

"You look as tired as I feel."

"Seeing you, wife, I am no longer weary. Tell me about your day."

Charlotte filled him in on what she'd been doing, and was pleased to hear him say she'd done such a great job. Who knew organizing archeological teams and villagers would be so similar?

With a look out the window, she pursed her lips. It was time. She couldn't put it off any longer. Who knew when they would have time together again? They had their chamber and the solar to themselves. But every other inch of the castle and its buildings were occupied with people. And someone always needed her or Henry for something. Charlotte wouldn't wait any longer. She owed it to her husband.

"I have something to tell you. Something I've wanted to tell you since the day you rescued me but haven't quite known how."

Henry put down his cup and came to stand next to her. They looked out at the water and the enemy beyond. He took her hands in his.

"Whatever it is, you may tell me. You know I would do anything within my power to aid you."

"I don't want you to think I've lost my wits. I just keep thinking if someone were to tell me what I'm about to tell you, I would think they were completely crazy. And I certainly wouldn't believe them."

"Charlotte. Look at me." Henry leaned forward and kissed her on the lips. "Whatever secrets you've been keeping, I am your husband and I will believe you."

Somehow hearing him say it, whether he would or not, made her feel so much lighter. Charlotte made a face and took a deep breath.

"Here goes. I'm from the future. From the year 2016. Almost seven hundred years from now."

Henry dropped her hands. He stared at her as if he were truly seeing her for the first time.

"The future? We found you washed up on the shore. 'Tis not possible."

She'd opened her mouth to start explaining when the damn door opened with a bang.

"My lord, my lady. Make haste. A messenger has arrived. He is not long for this world."

Hells bells. Charlotte wanted to run to the kitchens to see the messenger, but she also wanted to throw a serious tantrum like a two-year-old who'd gone two days without a nap. Just when she'd gotten her nerve up. Well, she'd waited this long, what was a few more hours?

Chapter Thirty-One

After supper, Charlotte was half-asleep in a chair when Henry came back. Groggy, she scrubbed a hand across her face.

There had been so much blood, she had to leave the room. As she gagged, she was afraid she'd barf and be a distraction. Even the healer couldn't save him. She'd patted Charlotte on the shoulder as she left the room.

"Blood takes getting used to, lady. Be of good cheer you do not find it so easy to bear."

She'd thanked the woman and run out of the room and into her chamber, where she took deep breaths out the window to clear the smell from her nose.

"Did he survive?"

Henry shook his head. "Nay. The messenger did not survive, though he did pass on a message."

"I don't understand. I thought during times of war, messengers were allowed to pass?"

"And allow information to get through to the enemy?

Nay, messengers are not given safe passage." He pulled her onto his lap, his breath warm against her ear. "The message was not written down for fear it would be discovered. The man memorized it. I did not forget what you told me. You swear you are from the future?"

"I am. Though I wouldn't blame you if you didn't believe me."

"'Tis odd; the messenger said Lady Blackford and Lady Falconburg are sisters. Lucy and Melinda Merriweather. They have your name. These are the sisters you search for? And if 'tis true, how can you be from the future?"

Charlotte wasn't sure she'd heard him correctly. "Did you say Lady Blackford and Lady Falconburg are my sisters? And we know where they are? But then why did they say they didn't have a third sister? We could have already gone to Falconburg. I would have been with them before the siege even started. You wouldn't have had to marry me."

Henry scowled. She ignored his look and jumped up, dancing around the room. "It doesn't matter. All that matters is I actually did it. Traveled through time and found my sisters." As the reality of her situation sank in, Charlotte slumped. "We must end the siege. I have to see them with my own eyes."

"'Tis been a long day. Tell me your tale from the beginning. As they come from...the future...they may not have wished to arouse suspicion by saying they had a third sister no one had ever met. Surely they will come to see for themselves it is truly you. Tell me your story, then I will tell you what I know of Lord Blackford and Lord Falconburg."

Charlotte was too agitated to sit. Instead, she paced around the room. She explained to Henry how Lucy's boyfriend tricked her into marriage and then tried to kill her. How Simon hired someone to kill she and Melinda.

"When Simon tried to murder my sister, I think that's when she went back in time. And when Melinda went to Falconburg by mistake." Charlotte grinned. "She couldn't find north if you pointed her in the right direction. I know somehow she went back in time."

"But how did they travel through time?"

"Hell if I know. The worst part? I told Melinda to get over it. That our sister was dead. I didn't believe her. And now I know. There's more to life than what we see with our own eyes. And time isn't a straight line; it's some kind of circle. Or a road with many paths."

"Melinda saw a painting in your time of your sister Lucy?"

"It's what sent her to England to look for answers."

Henry looked as if he were about to faint.

"William Brandon, Lord Blackford, is married to Lucy. He is a most ferocious fighter. They have five children." Henry cocked his head at her. "She is much older than you. William married her more than a score of years ago."

Charlotte's world tilted. "How can that be possible? She hasn't been gone that long." She was trying to figure out possible answers when Henry spoke again.

"And Melinda. James Rivers, Lord Falconburg, married her a few years ago. They call him the Red Knight for the blood staining his armor and sword crimson during battle.

I've never seen anyone fight like him. He fights until he collapses. Men would leave the field of battle rather than engage him."

"Melinda disappeared at Falconburg. That's where they found her car, but she hasn't been gone that long. There must be a way to get word to them. To tell them I'm here."

"They will know by now I have been making enquiries. Though they will not know why. We need my brother's armies." Henry was staring off into the distance with a look she had come to recognize. He was plotting.

"Falconburg is closest. If we could get a message there, James would send men to fight and dispatch messengers to my brothers and Lord Blackford."

Henry muttered, "We are using the gate at the east wall. 'Tis hidden and heavily guarded. We must be careful sending a messenger out; he will have no cover across the water. 'Tis our only hope."

Henry pulled her close and kissed her soundly. "I must have words with the men. When I return, I would like to hear more about this future."

She hugged him tight. "You believe me?"

He leaned back to look at her. "I believe you, wife. And I will see you reunited with your sisters."

She felt so much better since she'd told him. Charlotte sat back in the chair, drained. It was surprising how much energy it took to keep a secret and how tired you were once you finally told someone. She only meant to close her eyes for a moment.

Chapter Thirty-Two

Several of Hallsey's men tried in vain to swim across the water. Henry's archers ensured they did not get far. He was feeling the march of time. The trebuchet would arrive soon and the assault would begin. Henry dispatched another messenger. It would take him longer to evade the enemy. Perhaps several days to reach Falconburg.

The old woman's words came back to Henry. *Those you call friend will turn against you. A stranger will become more important to you than your own life. And when you see nothing but darkness ahead, look to the east.*

Blackford lay to the east, as did his brother Edward. Did that mean help would come in the shape of an army? Henry accepted Charlotte was the stranger, but what worried him most was who would turn against him? Had that bit of the prophecy already been fulfilled? Was it the three knights who betrayed him by not sounding the alarm when the enemy came? They were in league with Timothy and ran from the castle during the chaos. When this was over, Henry would send men to find them and they would pay for their treachery. Were there others?

The people's spirits were high, but it would not last once the assault started. And Henry would not be able to defend against the trebuchet. He prayed the walls would stand.

He chuckled as one of the archers bellowed an insult about swine and the man's dam before letting loose an arrow. The man to his left on the battlements released a bag, the stench making Henry breathe through his nose. He heard the curses as the refuse found its mark.

Today his wife was in the gardens. When she needed to think, she said feeling the earth between her fingers helped. Henry understood her need, for he liked to ride or to pace. And since he could not ride, he'd been pacing a great deal.

Standing there watching her, he was taken again by her beauty. Not just on the outside, but on the inside as well. As the sun hit her face, he realized with sudden clarity—he loved her. And the knowledge sent terror through him. As much as he tried to banish his parents from his thoughts, they intruded time and time again. Had they loved each other at one time? Henry could not remember, and thought not. But perchance they did before he and his brothers came along.

Children. Henry hadn't thought he would ever have children. But now? Married to Charlotte, he could picture a son and a daughter who looked like her.

"I was calling your name. You must be a million miles away."

Her odd mannerisms and speech made him accept her

story for truth. He wanted to know more about the future. Henry leaned close and whispered, "Can everyone in your time travel to the past? To the future?"

"I don't think this is something we should be talking about with so many people around. You saved me from being branded a witch once. I think we have enough to deal with without that coming up again."

"You are right, my lady. Let us go inside. For I wish to hear more about the future."

"So the two brothers try to kill my sister and I. I still can't figure out exactly how I traveled through time. I hope when I see Lucy and Melinda they will have figured it out. And no, people can't travel through time. I think it is a very rare ability. In my time, everyone hears information immediately. So I would know if other people had traveled through time."

"Tell me again about cars."

Charlotte laughed. He was fascinated by cars and trains, basically anything that moved.

"We sent men to the moon. To outer space, in the heavens."

He gaped at her. "Truly?" Henry looked up to the ceiling as if he could see through the stone and up to the sky. "Your time is a marvelous place." He frowned. "You must miss your time very much with so many marvels."

Charlotte pulled him close to her, putting her arms around him as they looked out the window. "I do not believe we can travel back to my time. I think if we could, my sisters would've already done it. I accepted this idea when I decided I would try to find them."

"Tell me again how it happened."

"The car I was in went over the cliff and hit the water. There was a terrible storm. I remember I was bleeding. I'd been hit from a piece from the other car—"

She trailed off then held out her arm. "This bracelet? I purchased it from a shop in London. When you gave it to me, I thought I would be sent back to my time. But somehow it didn't work."

Henry looked pale, and Charlotte braced herself in case he started to fall. But he recovered. "The bracelet? It exists in your time?" He looked at the bracelet as if seeing it for the first time. "It brought you to me."

"The more I think about it, I wonder if traveling through time has something to do with the storm, blood, and the bracelet. Somehow maybe the combination of those things sent me back. If something similar happened to Melinda and Lucy, we'll know, but it's not like it does us any good. We can't go back."

A while later she came up for air. Her husband sure could kiss. Charlotte started to mention the daggers, then stopped. What if Henry was planning to give them to her? If she mentioned them, something could happen. He might not give them to her. Or he might hide them, thinking they would find their way to her. Which might lead to her never buying them in the future or traveling through time. Because maybe it was the bracelet, or maybe the daggers? Unwilling to take the risk, she decided not to say anything and chance changing the way things were supposed to go.

"I would very much like to see your time."

"I think you would find it marvelous, and yet I prefer it here. My time has become so busy. People running to and fro; so much noise. The way the day unfolds is very different. This time suits my soul. I believe I am where I am meant to be. And my sisters are here. So I would not want to leave."

Charlotte touched his face. "And you are here. I am content." She leaned forward to kiss him, and after that there was no talking for quite a while.

Chapter Thirty-Three

All hours of the day and night, the enemy tried to cross the water. One made it to the wall but had nowhere to go. No handholds, nothing. Refuse and other stinky objects hit the walls, splashing into the water. It seemed they were having trouble with the trebuchet. She didn't know if a piece was missing or what, but it still wasn't assembled. Charlotte sent up a word of thanks, believing Aunt Pittypat was watching over them from the great beyond.

"Get some rest. You've been cooking nonstop for days." Charlotte patted the plump woman on the shoulder. Mrs. Benton looked like she was about to drop. As she started to protest, Charlotte stopped her.

"You have trained your helpers well. They know what they are to do. Go and rest."

"As you wish, my lady." The cook looked around the kitchen, and with a sigh of resignation put down her spoon.

Charlotte looked at the three women standing at attention. "Do not let our mistress of the kitchens be displeased. I know you will do well. We must keep everyone fed. If they are full they won't be in bad humor. Tomorrow you will change places with the next three women. And then Mrs. Benton will be back. We will continue taking turns until this is over. Those who do well and want to continue in the kitchens may do so if she agrees."

The women nodded. Charlotte could tell they were worried—she was too. But the best way to keep worry from taking over was to stay busy. She'd sorted out other groups of people to clean and others to do the wash and other assorted tasks. She knew how important it was to keep things clean and prevent infection. There was so much to do.

Right now, she missed her washer and dryer with a vengeance. Maybe if she described it, the men could come up with an old-fashioned crank to wring out the clothes, or a tub with spokes to function as an agitator. She'd seen them in antique stores. The rollers with a crank and tubs beneath. Surely a little thing like that wouldn't make a big difference to history?

As she walked out into the courtyard to check on people, three children ran up to her.

"My lady, we spotted a man in the water this morning. He did not make it across."

Charlotte smiled at them. "I knew all of you would be good lookouts. We must keep Ravenskirk safe."

She made her way to the lists to watch Henry and the men train. It had become her favorite way to start the day. At first she simply enjoyed watching them with the eye of her future self. Now, though...she appreciated the practice for what it was, always being ready to fight. When he finished, Henry walked over to her, wiping the sweat from his brow.

"The women believe you have commanded armies. You would've made a great warrior."

"I'm glad you think so. I find if I keep busy, I don't worry about what's happening beyond the walls. I think it helps the people too."

Henry leaned down and kissed her, to jeers from his men. He smiled at her. "They are envious I have such a comely wife."

Being together constantly, Charlotte felt she knew Henry better than she'd ever known anyone in her life. And knowing she loved him scared her. With everything currently happening, she was afraid. Afraid he would be taken from her. Afraid the messenger wouldn't make it and her sisters wouldn't know she was here. So much to worry about. Charlotte shook her head. She had to move again. Do something. Otherwise her thoughts would keep traveling down a dark path.

She hugged Henry. "I want to check on Father Riley." The man was timid and shy at the best of times. With the siege going on, he could barely bring himself to leave the chapel.

"Take him some food. Talk with him. He says the sound of your voice calms him."

"I will. See you later." The priest was a nice enough man. She wondered why he was always so afraid.

Charlotte packed a basket in the kitchens, stopped to sort out two women fighting over eggs, and made her way to the chapel.

"Hello? Father Riley? I brought you food and ale."

The man trembled as he sat up. How on earth could he sleep on the hard wood?

"Thank you, lady. I don't remember the last time I ate."

She sat down next to him and waited until he'd eaten a few bites before she asked, "Why do you refuse to leave the chapel?"

"There are so many people outside. Too many people gathered together make me nervous." He looked at her, his head bobbing up and down. "More nervous than I usually am, lady. You see, when I was a boy, I did not want to be a priest. But my father said it would be so, and here I am."

"I understand. When you were a child, what did you want to be when you grew up?"

The man's face brightened, and it was the first time Charlotte didn't think he looked like a little mouse about to be pounced on by a big, hungry cat.

"I wanted to raise bees and make mead. Bees make me happy."

"Their honey tastes delicious. Would you like me to talk to Henry? I'm sure he would agree to let you keep bees and make mead. He's always looking to fill his storerooms full of spirits. And I know we could use our own supply of honey. I could make more cakes."

The little man looked horrified. "Nay, lady. Lord Ravenskirk would be most displeased. He must have a priest in the chapel."

"Henry will not be displeased. I heard one of the young men talking about how he wished to take his vows and become a priest. Perhaps you could help him and he could be our priest? Then you could tend your bees. Would that please you?"

"More than you know, lady. I cannot thank you enough. Though if Timothy hears of it, he will tell the bishop and make trouble for you both."

As if saying the rotten man's name out loud conjured it, there was a loud rumble. Charlotte looked up to see dust falling down, and the roof was shaking. Had their enemy finished putting together the trebuchet?

Rubble rained down and Charlotte grabbed the priest by the arm. "We have to get out of here." They ran for the door, almost reaching it before the roof collapsed. Charlotte yanked the priest by his robe as hard as she could. Turning back to the front of the chapel, they dove for the stone altar.

She came to coughing. There was rubble and dust all around them. As Charlotte peered around, she could make out the walls of the chapel. When she looked up, she saw daylight. The entire roof had come down, practically on their heads.

The stone altar had saved their lives. It was a heavy piece and carved with animals all the way around. She touched a finger to her pounding head. There was a bump on her forehead and her finger came away red. A piece of the roof must have hit her. Father Riley was moaning softly.

"Are you hurt?"

He whimpered. "My leg is trapped under the stone. Perhaps God does not want me to leave the priesthood."

"Nonsense. The chapel is old and the roof must have weakened. It had nothing to do with God. We must do what we feel called to do. You feel called to raise bees. Are they not God's creatures?"

The man nodded. "Mayhap you are right, lady."

"Let me see if I can get out of here and find help." Charlotte tried to push against the stone, but it wouldn't move. It seemed they were trapped under the altar. Everywhere she looked, nothing but rubble.

With so many people about, all she had to do was wait. Though patience wasn't one of her virtues. Thank goodness Father Riley was with her, otherwise she probably would have been curled up in a ball having a panic attack. But worrying over him kept her anxiety at bay.

Charlotte called out, "Hello? Can anyone hear me? We're trapped under the altar." And she kept yelling, for she could hear voices. And among the voices she heard Henry. He would come for her. He was her knight in shining armor.

Chapter Thirty-Four

A loud boom startled Henry. He turned in time to watch the roof of the chapel collapse. What happened? The trebuchet was not yet working.

"Charlotte and Father Riley are in there," he bellowed as he ran.

All the battles he'd fought, all the danger he'd experienced in his score and seven years, nothing had prepared him for the feeling of watching the roof collapse while the woman he loved was inside.

He loved her. Henry had broken the vow he'd made to himself. He muttered, "Let the priest live. I have need of his counsel."

Garrison knights and villagers ran to aid him.

"Keep guards along the walls, but everyone else clear the rubble. Charlotte and Father Riley are trapped inside."

Henry listened. A weak voice called out for help. She was alive. His heart rejoiced.

"Charlotte!" Henry bellowed. "I am coming for you."

When the roof fell, it took down the front door and wall. They would have to clear away the rubble piece by piece to get in.

Addie looked up at him, tears running down her dirt-streaked face. "My lady is trapped inside. I should have been with her. I want to help." She gestured to a group of children behind her. "We all want to help."

"All of you can pick up the small pieces and put them in piles near the walls." It took everything he had, but Henry forced a smile to his face. "We'll use them to throw over the walls. Each of you can throw a bucket on the enemy when we're done. Would you like that?"

The children cheered, slightly lifting his spirits. They got to work quickly running back and forth, picking up the smallest pieces, leaving Henry and his men along with the others to move the larger stones.

He stretched, wiping the sweat from his brow. They'd labored through the morning and cleared the front of the chapel.

Henry pulled his tunic over his head. He accepted a bucket of water from the well, dumped it over his head, and shook his hair. Much better.

"My lord, one of the men heard voices. It sounds as if they are near the altar. There's a large stone trapping them. We're going to need many men to move it."

The men surrounded the stone from the roof. They took hold and pushed with all their might, grunting with the effort. As he strained, Henry felt the stone shift. It shifted a bit more, and with a great heave, he and the men lifted it enough to move it. "To the left, man."

Agonizingly slowly, they moved the stone. It was almost clear when two of the men from the village stumbled, losing their grip. Henry cursed as the edge raked down his thigh. Warmth trickled down his leg. There'd be time to tend to it later.

"Make ready. Put it down." The stone hit the dirt, sending up a cloud of dust. Henry and the men stood doubled over, hands on their knees, panting from the effort. But they had done it. There was no time to rest. His voice rough, Henry said, "I'm coming, my love."

The children cleared the smaller stones. There was an opening. One of the children called out, "I see them." The boy was small enough to crawl through the opening, his excited voice carrying to them.

"Our lady is unharmed. But Father Riley believes his leg broken. There's a big stone on his leg and our lady cannot move it."

Everyone continued to work, clearing the rest of the stone. It was late afternoon by the time they reached the altar. Henry pushed forward. "Charlotte. Where are you?"

"Under the altar. I'm coming." As he held his breath, she emerged, covered in dust, looking like a corpse. She wobbled. He swung her up into his arms.

"You saved me."

"I told you, I will always be there." Henry wiped his eye. "'Tis dust from the rubble, nothing more," he said gruffly.

"Father Riley is trapped. His leg is broken."

Henry turned so she could see the stone being removed.

Men from the village carried Father Riley out.

Henry put his hand on the priest's shoulder. "I am glad you are alive."

The priest replied without stuttering, without trembling, his voice strong and clear. Henry gaped at the man.

"While we were trapped, God spoke to me. He told me I am not meant to be a priest. I will tend to the bees and make mead." Father Riley pulled on Henry's arm. Henry put Charlotte down. They both leaned in to hear what the man had to say.

"Please, my lady. This is for his ears only."

Charlotte held up her hands and backed away. "By all means."

Henry leaned close to the priest.

"He gave me a message for you, my lord. Your vow is not broken. It was never a true vow, only a childish thought. You will not repeat the past." The man fainted as Henry caught him.

"We will need a new priest." Royce slapped Henry on the back. "I love mead." Then his face turned grave. "Blood. Are you injured, my lady?"

Charlotte patted herself. "I am unharmed. Just scared." She looked down and gasped. "Henry, that's your blood, not mine."

He was having a difficult time hearing her. "The stone cut me when we were moving it. 'Tis naught but a scratch."

He swept her up into his arms again, carrying her inside the castle and up to their chamber. Henry laid her on the bed.

"A bath is being prepared. I will have food sent up." As he turned to go, he could see two of everything. Henry blinked to clear his vision, but 'twas no use. Was he going blind? It was his last thought before he fell.

Chapter Thirty-Five

Charlotte didn't know how anything else could possibly go wrong. Henry went down like a marionette with its strings cut. She leapt from the bed, tried to rouse him, and, with no response, ran into the hallway. Chester leaned against the wall, arms crossed over his chest.

"Henry fell. There's blood everywhere and I can't get him to the bed."

Chester bellowed down the hallway, and two more men came running. They lifted Henry, Chester swept off the desk with one swoop of his arm, and the men laid him on top.

"Why the desk?" She looked to the bed. "Oh, so he doesn't bleed all over the sheets."

A sound like thunder made her cringe.

Chester looked out the window. "Do not worry, lady. The walls are thick. They will hold."

"I hope so."

Henry was mumbling and moaning. When she touched his forehead, the heat radiated through her fingers.

Charlotte looked down to see the entire left side of his body was wet. She touched his hose, her fingers coming away bright red.

Chester stepped forward, pulled a blade from his belt, and slit Henry's hose up the leg. She clapped a hand over her mouth, her entire body going cold as if she'd gone swimming in the ocean in winter.

His thigh was cut from above his knee to his groin. The wound looked dirty. She could see small pebbles and dirt inside the flesh.

Charlotte ran to the garderobe, barely making it in time as she threw up. She'd thought she was getting better at handling the sight of blood, had helped patch up the men and villagers' minor scratches. But seeing such an awful wound on someone you loved was completely different.

Grateful there were rags to wipe her mouth, Charlotte splashed water over her face and came back into the chamber, trying to breathe through her mouth. A tiny old woman, a skilled healer from what Charlotte had seen, was examining Henry, mumbling.

"Heat water over the fire and bring me clean cloths." She rummaged in the sack she'd brought with her, and the smell of herbs filled the air.

"Tell me what I can do to help." Charlotte was shaking so badly she wasn't sure how much help she would be, but Henry had saved her life and she would do everything she could to help him.

"You are his lady. Speak softly to him as I clean the wound." She motioned to Chester and the other men. "We will require a fourth man to hold him still."

Chester blanched, and Charlotte thought her face must look the same. Without a word, he turned and left the room. It seemed like seconds later he returned with another man.

"I have informed the captain. We must not let everyone know how grave his injuries are."

The woman poured the herbs into the water. A man brought the alcohol she'd requested. She looked up at them. "Hold him still."

The healer opened the bottle, the pungent fumes filling the room. When she poured the liquid over the wound, Henry arched up, screaming, before he fell back again, unconscious.

One of the men looked nervous. "Is it the fever sickness?"

Chester rolled his eyes. "'Tis his leg, dolt."

To know Henry was in so much pain and she couldn't make it better, she wished there was a hospital nearby—and with that thought, Charlotte remembered. The antibiotics.

As soon as she was alone, she would get them and give them to Henry. This definitely qualified as an emergency.

The woman cleaned the wound and Charlotte had to look away. Henry cried out, cursed in several languages, making the men chuckle, and then fell silent again. It was repeated over and over. Charlotte wondered where she'd learned to do such a thing. As if the healer heard her thoughts, she met her eyes and said, "An old priest in a monastery told me about foul humors that enter the body. He said using alcohol on needles or anything that touches a wound will prevent foul humors."

Was another traveler here? Or simply a learned man? Likely she would never know, but the thought wouldn't leave her mind. If she and her sisters had managed to travel through time, why wouldn't there be others? It was too bad there wasn't a way for them all to come together and talk. There had to be so much they could learn from each other.

Candles were brought into the room and lit as the old lady stitched up the wound and bandaged it. Charlotte dipped the cloth into cool water and placed it on Henry's forehead, repeating as his fever warmed the rag. One of the kitchen girls brought food to the chamber. Her stomach rumbled. When had she last eaten? Maybe breakfast?

After the woman finished, she patted Charlotte on the arm. "Make him drink a cup every few hours. He may not keep it down, but you must keep trying. Three days. That is all I can do."

Charlotte took the woman's hands. "I don't know how to thank you. What payment is required?"

The woman gave her a quizzical look. "Payment?"

Charlotte nodded. The healer smiled, showing a few missing teeth. "Lord Ravenskirk has always been good to me. There is no money required. I shelter here while the enemy is outside. Though perhaps I might harvest herbs from the gardens?"

"Of course. Take whatever you need." Charlotte hoped she wasn't overstepping her bounds. "You said you live in the village. We don't have a healer in residence. Would you consider living here and being the castle healer?"

The woman beamed at her. "I have a daughter, and she has three bairns. They would live with me."

"Yes. They are most welcome. We will find proper accommodations for everyone once this is over with."

"You are a strong woman, Lady Ravenskirk. Our lord has chosen well." She gathered up her things and shuffled toward the door. She turned and looked back at Charlotte. "Call if you have need of me."

Charlotte looked to the men in the room. "Thank you all for helping. I do not want to alarm the people. Too many already know. Can we keep this quiet?"

Chester said, "They know he was injured, but not how greatly. I will say he is resting and you are attending to him, lady. The rest are loyal and will not gossip."

"I'll stay with him. You must be hungry. Go and eat."

The men quietly left the room, and Charlotte was finally alone with him. Henry was still unconscious. Every once in a while he would moan and call out. She dipped a ladle into the cauldron, pouring the brew into a cup. She could put the antibiotics in the drink.

Certain she was alone at last, Charlotte went to the trunk at the bottom of the bed. She opened it and pulled out her messenger bag. It seemed so long ago she'd left North Carolina for London. She dumped the contents on the bed and sorted through them, looking for a small cloth bundle.

"No, no, no." She unwrapped the small glass vial. She'd been so certain Henry would be fine when she gave him antibiotics. But somehow the lid must've come loose, and she was now looking at what looked like cloudy seawater.

She twisted the lid off and sniffed. It smelled salty. Was it possible any of the antibiotic was left?

She touched her finger to the liquid and then to her tongue. It tasted salty, not bitter, as she'd expected it to. She looked at Henry. Likely it wouldn't kill him. Before she could think about it too long, Charlotte dumped it into the mug. *If you're up there listening, Aunt Pittypat, please don't let him die.*

Charlotte lifted his head up. "Wake up, Henry. You must wake."

His eyes fluttered and opened partway. She held the cup to his mouth. "It's going to taste terrible, but you have to drink it."

She poured half of the brew down his throat before he started coughing and sputtering. As she waited for the fit to subside, she pleaded, "Just a little bit more."

She got the rest of it down and sat back exhausted. All she could do now was wait. Thank goodness it was growing dark. The assault on the walls had stopped for the night. Charlotte had heard the boom every time something from the trebuchet hit the walls. How quickly she'd grown used to the thundering. Now the absence of sound made her notice it had stopped. If they didn't find a way out of this, eventually the walls would fall. And she didn't want to think on the hand-to-hand battle that would come after.

Chapter Thirty-Six

It had been three days since the assault on the walls. Charlotte's nerves were frayed with the constant worry the wall would fall and they would face a battle. She knew the big history events, knew the Black Plague happened during this century, but she'd never really given much thought to small skirmishes or battles. She naïvely assumed it wouldn't happen to her. And now here she was in the middle of a small war.

At times like this, she missed the modern world. Missed her boring job, people grouchy as they waiting in line at the grocery store, judging the contents of other shoppers' baskets.

She'd taken a bath and dressed in clean clothes for the first time in—well, she couldn't remember, but knew she smelled pretty ripe when she finally had time for a bath. Charlotte sat down next to Henry, taking his hand in hers. It was funny. Coming to love someone after you were already married to them. But that was exactly what had happened to her. She had a crush on him at the beginning, which developed into friendship, and then into something more. He married her out of his chivalrous knightly vows. But now...she thought he was coming to love her too.

Henry's eyes fluttered and he tried to sit up.

"Wait. Let me help you." She thought he looked much better. "Don't fall over while I get you something to drink."

He managed a small smile. "Married such a short time and you're already plaguing me."

For the first time since he'd fallen ill, she grinned. "I've been so worried about you. I should kill you for making me worry so much."

"Tell me all that has happened. I must see to the men." He put his feet down on the floor. Charlotte stopped him, a hand on his shoulder. She could see the pulse fluttering at his throat.

"You are not going anywhere. You will stay in this bed until the healer says you are well enough to get up."

She arranged the covers around him and handed him a cup of ale.

"I quite like this shrewish wife of mine."

She rolled her eyes. "By the way, I offered the healer, along with her daughter and three children, a place at the castle. She saved your life and I thought we should have someone here. I hope that was all right?"

"You are Lady Ravenskirk. 'Tis your right to bring those we need to the castle."

She climbed into bed beside him. He rested his head in her lap while she told him what had been happening while he was healing. As she finished talking, another assault on the walls sent dust and small pieces of mortar falling from the ceiling. She cringed.

"I'm worried the walls won't hold."

"They are twenty feet thick. They will hold." Though he didn't look totally convinced.

He finished the ale and put on his Prince Charming smile. "I'm hungry." She gave him bread and cheese. He arched a brow. "I want a proper meal with meat."

"You'll throw up if I give you that. You haven't eaten in days. Eat this first and keep it down. Then I'll bring you a proper meal."

He pouted. "And two of the small cakes?"

She kissed him on the cheek. "Yes. If you're a good patient."

Charlotte was telling Henry every detail she could remember since he'd been ill when Royce strode into the room.

"Henry. 'Tis good to see you awake. We were most worried."

"You worry like an old woman. I am fine and will see you in the lists tomorrow."

His captain grinned. "I'll knock you on your arse."

"See what I must put up with? No one fears me."

"A messenger made it through the enemy. He shot an arrow with a message attached over the wall. Liam found it. He is waiting in the water by the corner of the east wall and will make the swim tonight."

"How do we know he's not a spy for Hallsey?" Charlotte

asked.

"The note ended with *We miss Holden but we miss you more.*"

Charlotte started to cry. "My sisters know I'm here. It's from them. Holden is Holden Beach. Where I'm from."

Henry stroked her cheek. "Help me up. I would have speech with the man."

She wanted to protest, but on second thought, it was important. She looked to Royce. "I can't lift him; he weighs a ton. Can you help me get him up?"

Henry grumbled then shut his mouth. "He can help me up, but he is not helping me dress like some small child."

His captain laughed. "You fight like a wee child. Why shouldn't I dress you?"

They traded insults as Henry stood on his feet swaying back and forth like a drunk. He found his center and stood steady. Tears rolled down her face.

"What's amiss? Why do you weep, my love?"

"I'm so happy to see you up and well. You don't know how I worried about you. Don't ever do that to me again."

Royce backed out of the room, giving them privacy. Henry opened his arms, and Charlotte went to him as he held her tight.

"The priest told me I would not repeat the past. And my vow to myself is not binding. I have been so worried I would end up like my parents, hating who I married, that I vowed never to marry."

He kissed her lightly on the lips. "Rescuing you from the rubble took my fear away. I was so worried about losing you. I want you to know I love you. I think I fell in love with you the moment I saw your blue toes on the beach. I love you, Charlotte. Body and soul. I belong to you and I will love you all the days of my life."

Charlotte started to cry again, and then the hiccups began. "I love you too, Henry. I've known it for a while but didn't know how to say it. I too never thought love was something I would have. It seems we are perfectly suited to each other, husband."

"Say it again."

"What?"

"Husband."

Charlotte smiled. "Husband. My Henry. I love you more than all the stars in the sky."

He stumbled slightly as they made their way down to the hall. He kept her close, an arm wrapped tightly around her waist. Charlotte wasn't sure if it was for him or for her. Either way, she didn't care. She was happy. And soon she would be reunited with her sisters. Even the relentless assault shaking the walls couldn't ruin her mood.

Chapter Thirty-Seven

"Gosh, you're huge."

Melinda put a hand on her belly. "I'm due next month, so I can't travel. It is so good to see you, Lucy."

How was it possible that all three of them would be together again? For Melinda had no doubt it was Charlotte who had been asking about the two of them. Her baby sister was in trouble, and she'd move heaven and earth to help her.

"Can you believe Charlotte came looking for us? I wonder what happened to bring her here." Lucy followed Melinda into the solar.

"How are the kids?"

"My youngest is already sixteen. The oldest is twenty-two, and I'm hopeful we'll have a wedding to plan soon. I don't see them as often as I'd like, but they're all doing well."

"Wait until Charlotte sees you. I bet she'll be as shocked as I was. Of course, I've been here three years. Won't she be surprised to hear that as well? I wonder why the difference in time?"

"It was the first day of summer. Maybe all the New Age books had it right. The first day of every season has some kind of magical power. Gives you more control as to when you land in time," Lucy said.

"I just wonder what kind of ordeal Charlotte went through to get here. It wasn't like it was easy for either one of us." The baby kicked, and Melinda smiled. "I wish I could go with you guys. Promise me you'll bring Charlotte back so I can see her."

"Pinky swear."

Melinda poured. She was drinking watered-down wine. "I wish we could've pulled all this together sooner. Who knew it took so long to gather armies?"

"Speaking of armies—where are our husbands?" Lucy stood and looked out the window. "I see them. They're in the courtyard. As tall as they are, it's easy to spot them."

"If Charlotte can hold on for a few more days, we'll have the cavalry there."

"It will probably be a week by the time the rest of the Thornton brothers arrive. Charlotte couldn't have picked a better guy. I hear Henry is as hot as he is charming." Melinda wondered, did Henry know about John? She hadn't even told Lucy. She'd kept his secret, as he asked. As had James. It would be interesting to meet Edward, Robert, and Christian. Other than the king, the Thornton brothers, her husband, and Lucy's husband were the most powerful men in the realm.

"Lord Hallsey has balls to think he can take on all of us," Lucy said, echoing what Melinda was thinking.

"Let's just hope we're not too late."

"Let me help get things ready. With so many men here, you'll run yourself ragged. And you need to take care of yourself during this last month." Lucy hugged her again. "I'm so happy our baby sis is here."

"The Merriweather sisters, reunited."

Besieged. The enemy camped outside had taken to hurling dead animals over the castle walls, hoping to spread disease. If they got out of this okay, the only good that would come of it was that Charlotte might be prepared for some of the horribly icky stuff that was bound to come with the Black Plague.

She planned to talk to her sisters. Would it make sense for all of them to leave Europe? To find someplace safe until the plague passed?

Henry had decided that once this was all over they would expand the moat. It was only fifty feet across, and the trebuchet had a range of almost nine hundred feet. She knew they couldn't make it that wide, but they could at least make it wider and a bit more difficult. He also planned to make the land closer to the castle more uneven. Beyond that, they needed the fields and orchards for food production.

Charlotte had never been so thankful they had the two freshwater wells. The one inside the courtyard and the one within the castle walls. She couldn't imagine starving to death or dying of thirst.

She had to hope her sisters would be coming soon. Henry was certain they had sent word to his brothers, and they would be coming as well. He had a funny look on his face when he said they'd be arriving from the east. And then he reminded her of what the old woman had told him in the wood.

It seemed she had some kind of sight into the future. For she had predicted he and Charlotte meeting and falling in love as well as help coming from the east. Assuming help did come. The only thing that had not come to pass was a friend who would no longer be a friend. Unless it was Timothy and his three henchmen? But she wasn't sure, and that made her more nervous than anything else.

She would be counting the hours, even knowing it would take them probably double or triple the time to travel, given the enemy camped outside the gates. So they were looking at anywhere from three days to a week before help arrived. There was a large crack in the western wall. And Henry was concerned it wasn't going to hold. They were trying to brace it, but the repeated assaults were doing their job.

Had she comes so far, found Henry, fallen in love, and found her sisters, only to have it all snatched away? Charlotte didn't think the fates would be so cruel. She had to believe they would make it through this. And her old self would've thought it horrible to think such a thought, but the medieval Charlotte, Lady Ravenskirk—she wanted Lord Hallsey's head on a pike outside the gates.

Chapter Thirty-Eight

Lucy was in full-scale organization mode. With her sister about ready to pop, she offered to take control. She'd never seen so many men gathered together.

There were tents set up inside the castle walls and outside. It looked like a city of fabric. She was glad the weather was nice so the men wouldn't be uncomfortable. Then again, they were probably used to harsh conditions.

She'd lived in the past for more than twenty years, and in all that time hadn't seen a battle up close and personal. Lucy hoped she would get through life without ever seeing one, but it seemed it was not to be so. She would do anything to help her sisters. How long had Charlotte been in the past? How did she get here and what was the deal between she and Henry? Though given the good looks of his brothers, Charlotte must be pretty happy.

Lucy had never seen so many good-looking men all in one place. The only one who stood out was Melinda's husband, James. And even with his scars he was still attractive. She had to admit they were handsome, yet there was something about them that made you take a step back. To know these were serious men.

"Lady Blackford? Allow me to introduce myself."

"Please, call me Lucy."

The man made her a small bow. He had blonde hair, blue eyes, and a very intense look.

"I am Edward Thornton." He pointed to the other men. "My brothers, Robert and Christian."

The men greeted her warmly.

"It's easy to tell you are brothers. Thank you for coming. I haven't met your brother Henry yet. And I haven't seen my sister Charlotte in a very long time. I don't mean to sound rude, but do you think you'll be leaving soon?"

Christian laughed. "You and Melinda may not look alike, but you certainly sound alike. I think she made Edward's ears bleed when we arrived."

Lucy felt the skin on her cheeks heat up.

"Melinda can be bossy when she's cranky. And she's cranky all the time, given she's due to give birth in a month."

All the men nodded, and Robert said, "Thank the gods I'm not married." Both brothers nodded. Lucy wanted to warn them to be careful. Tempt fate with a statement like that and you might find yourself married quicker than you think. It was always those who said they wouldn't that ended up marrying first.

"We travel with eight hundred men. We had to leave men behind to guard the castle, but I believe we will quite overwhelm Lord Hallsey's paltry forces. He has been after Ravenskirk for years."

Robert said, "Our father used to laugh about taking the castle from him. He's wanted it back ever since. Henry should've killed him when he had the chance."

"So in answer to your question, lady. We will be leaving in two days," Christian said.

Two days. She could manage two more days. But how was Charlotte holding up?

Henry was moving around better. His leg didn't seem to pain him as much. She didn't think she'd ever know if the saltwater antibiotic solution worked or if it was the herbal brew the healer made that broke his fever. Charlotte spent time with the healer, following her around, learning what she could. The woman knew her stuff. She treated all types of wounds. Everything from broken fingers to cuts and lacerations.

Some of Henry's best archers had taken out some of their enemy. But Hallsey had hired mercenaries. And as she saw the increase in the number of men outside the castle walls, her heart sank.

They'd had quiet for a few days after a piece broke loose from the trebuchet. Apparently they had to send for a replacement, and it had arrived today. So the head-pounding assault would begin again. Charlotte was obsessed with the west wall. She walked by it at least ten times a day to reassure herself it was still standing and not about to fall. There were several cracks in it, but it seemed to be holding.

The rest of her time was spent reassuring people things would be okay, helping plan out meals to feed the group, and rotating daily tasks for everyone. Keeping busy was the only thing that kept her sane.

At night she and Henry would talk about their childhoods and lives before they met. She told him all about Aunt Pittypat. How much she missed her, how much her eccentric aunt would've loved this grand adventure to another time.

Henry told her about his family. And she understood why he'd been so opposed to marriage. As miserable as his parents had been, it was a wonder he'd been able to overcome the fear.

She understood how fear could grab hold, twist your thoughts irrationally, and make it so that you lost all perspective. When something happened to you, it was easy to lose perspective. Standing outside, watching someone else, it was easy to have perspective on their situation.

You never really knew what you would do until something happened. You might have an idea of how you would react when things hit the fan, but it was only when something bad happened that you found out the kind of person you were deep inside.

Henry told her all about his brother John. His brother

would've been thirty-two this year. He seemed to be the wild child in the family. Henry told her John had been caught in bed with the king's mistress. He escaped death, but his poor decision cost them dearly. While John lost his title, lands, and money, the rest of the family suffered heavy fines. The king also saw fit to confiscate choice lands and titles. But over the past ten years, serving as mercenaries and winning tourneys, they had regained their wealth and status.

Then he laughed and said he wished his father, as horrible as he was, were alive now. He would take great pleasure in yelling back and forth with Hallsey. The younger Hallsey was much like the old.

Charlotte gave the man credit. Every morning he came out and bellowed at the walls for Henry and his men to come out and fight. When Henry would yell back that he would fight the man in single combat, the man always laughed and said no, he preferred a battle. He did not believe in fighting fair.

Henry assured her they would see the army coming. He estimated there would be close to a thousand men. And Charlotte hoped with all her heart there would not be a terrible battle. That Hallsey would see he was outnumbered and leave quietly. She didn't want men to lose their lives. Except for Hallsey. He'd instigated the whole thing and needed to pay. She had grown to despise him.

Chapter Thirty-Nine

The next day, Charlotte was outside checking on the dried fruit. Several women set up racks that allowed air to circulate freely around the fruit. The sun shining down would then dry it out, preserving it for the winter. It was fascinating to watch, and she had to laugh when one of the small children would run in and try to snatch a piece. The women were diligent and usually caught the offender before they got away with the treat.

One of the other women showed her how she made elderberry and dandelion wine. Charlotte wrinkled her nose, remembering the dandelion wine she'd had with the history buffs. This, though, had something else added to it to make it taste better. She was about to ask the woman what it was when she saw something move near the rubble of the chapel.

A great deal of the stone had been stacked into piles to be reused. The pieces that were deemed unable to be reused had been thrown over the wall at the enemy. She looked again. There was someone moving around the chapel near the altar where she had been trapped.

She was walking over to look when someone called her name. She stopped to deal with a minor crisis involving an argument over a couple of chickens, and when she returned there was no one near the chapel. It must've been one of the men checking on the stone.

The architect. What was his name again? He was drawing up plans for the new chapel. The village man who would take over as priest was working with him. Charlotte thought the young man was nice and would be a good addition.

Father Riley had been busy making plans for his bees. She didn't know if they were overly ambitious or not. But given what he was calculating, they would have a great deal of honey, and of course the mead. She loved honey and could think of all kinds of uses for it.

At dinner that night, she looked at all the people crowded into the hall and smiled. While things might be pretty bad outside, she was grateful for the sense of closeness and community.

Charlotte looked around the hall, trying to view her home through the eyes of a stranger. So many people thought medieval times were terribly stinky and dirty. And yes, there were a lot of people who didn't bathe frequently, and she'd heard stories of filthy halls and homes. But Ravenskirk was lovely.

The great hall had whitewashed walls, some painted with scenes of animals, flowers, and, of course, battle scenes.

There were tapestries on the walls featuring bees, butterflies, flowers, and animals. The floors were covered with patterned tiles. There were white tablecloths on the trestle tables, with ceramic wine jugs and ale flagons up and down all the tables. The table where they sat had cushions on the benches, a silver salt cellar, and beautifully enameled silver drinking cups. And the clothing. The embroidery was amazing. The cost would be astronomical in her time, and she constantly admired the designs on her dresses. The girls and women with the ability to do such work blew her away.

"It's funny, when I thought about traveling through time, I thought I'd have to sleep on a lumpy straw mattress." Charlotte ran her hands over the bed. "Instead we have straw but a feather mattress on top. Linen sheets, feather pillows, woolen blankets, and a beautifully embroidered bedspread. I feel like a queen."

Henry snorted. "The king and the queen have much fancier linens than we."

"I bet they have a fancier garderobe too."

"Ours is as good. The seats are covered with cloth; the waste falls down the chute into a barrel, which is emptied into the pit. We have plenty of wool and linen to wipe, along with a jug of water to wash when done. What more could you ask for?"

His eyes twinkled and he picked her up, spinning her around.

"Oh yes, your wonderfully hot showers. Endless hot water. You turn a knob and it comes out at your command. I would love to see such marvels."

A knock sounded. "Apologies. There is a matter requiring your attention." Chester had a scowl on his face. This couldn't be good.

"I will be back soon, wife."

Henry followed the man out into the hallway. "What is amiss?"

"Three men were captured coming out of the floor of the chapel near the altar. Did you know there is a passage underneath the chapel?"

Henry shook his head. He had never heard tell of passages in the castle.

"I sent two men down. The passage runs the length of the castle, almost like another floor. We found two more men. They died fighting."

"Have we questioned them?"

"Aye. It seems Timothy is back. He told them if they waited until the changing of the guard in the middle of the night when the man were tired, they could slip into the water and they would find an old gate at the northwest corner. It would be unlocked and they could gain entrance to the passage underneath the castle."

Henry swore viciously. "It seems we have a traitor within, for someone would've had to unlock the gate. Show me."

He followed the man outside to the chapel. At the altar stone, the man felt around, and Henry watched as he reached underneath the lip of the altar. He heard a click and a stone opened in the floor. There were stairs leading down. He could see the light. Someone had already put torches along the walls to light the way.

Part of him was excited. There would be more storage room in case of a longer siege. He could move all of the spirits down here. He would also have to make sure the gate was constantly guarded. He didn't want to close it up; it could prove useful as an escape route.

They explored the passageway and the rooms but found no trace of anyone else.

"How many men came with them?"

"Seven, my lord, including Timothy."

"So we're missing Timothy and likely a guard with him. Damn the man for returning."

While Henry had never counted Timothy as a friend, he thought the woman's prophecy rang true. For Henry had allowed the man to live in his home, treated him as one of his own. This latest betrayal should not have come as a surprise, yet it cut deeply. Chester led him to what looked like a pool of water. Henry could see steps leading down.

"At the bottom is the gate." He pointed to a ring of heavy keys on the wall. "These were in the lock on the gate." Chester nodded to the man standing at attention.

"We will keep the gate guarded at all times, my lord."

Henry had a bad feeling. "What is he plotting? Timothy

could not replace the bridge on his own."

Chester looked grim. "He could kill the man at the gate while everyone is asleep, allowing men to swim over. They could then enter and put the new bridge in place."

Henry swore again. "Kill the remaining men you captured and throw their bodies over the wall. Then take four or five men and search the castle. Do not alarm the people. I do not want Timothy to know we are coming for him."

The man nodded, a grim look on his face. Henry made his way back. Pressing under the lip of the altar again closed it and opened the stone. It was clever, and he wanted to examine it further when everything was over. The chapel was quite old. Henry wondered about the man who built it.

As he made his way up the stairs back toward his chamber, he heard a scream. It was Charlotte. He took the remaining steps two at a time, bursting into the room.

She stood over a man covered in muck. Henry caught the smell and started to gag. The man must have climbed up through the chute in the garderobe.

"Are you injured?"

Her hand was shaking, and she looked furious. "I'm fine. I went into the garderobe and heard a noise. You cannot imagine how surprised I was to see a man appear out of the stone seat." She burst into hysterical laughter.

"He had the fabric ring around his neck. It looked like it was stuck. He smelled so bad and looked like some kind of monster out of a bad horror movie. I think I stood there for a minute before I realized it was real."

Henry had left his wife unguarded. He would never make the same mistake again.

"I took the pitcher and smashed him over the head. He started to get up and I took your sword—you have no idea how freaking heavy that thing is. I lifted it over my head and stabbed him with it. Right where they showed me. He made a funny noise and hasn't moved since."

Her teeth started to chatter. "I've never killed a man before. Well, except for the man who tried to kill me when I ran him off the road. But that was different; his car went over the cliff. He didn't actually die by my hand, and not up close. It's different when they're close," she whispered.

Aye, it was. Henry was full of sorrow that she now knew this truth for herself. Charlotte trembled, pale as her chemise. Henry bellowed for Liam then picked his wife up, holding her tight. If he had lost her...

"Have this mess cleaned up. Tell Chester we found the sixth man. And have spiced wine sent up for Charlotte."

He rocked her back and forth, mumbling into her hair. She sniffed and wiped her nose, looking up at him. The corners of her mouth twitched, and she started laughing again then hiccuping.

"Can you imagine if I had sat down when he came up from the toilet?" She laughed and wept at the same time.

Not knowing what to do, Henry stroked her back, speaking softly. The more he thought about what she said, the more he tried not to laugh. Charlotte saw him and touched the corner of his mouth.

"Go ahead. It is rather funny."

Henry threw back his head and laughed. He could imagine going to take a piss and finding you weren't alone.

"I don't think I'll ever sit down again without checking first," she said, and they both dissolved into hysterics.

Chapter Forty

Breakfast the next morning was porridge, cheese, bread, and ale. After she'd gotten over her hysterics, Henry told her what had transpired. Charlotte jumped at every noise, picturing Timothy coming for her. She knew how much he hated her, and was afraid it was personal. What was with men trying to kill her?

Charlotte was discussing the meals for the rest of the day when the entire castle shook, the sound deafening. As she stood there trying to make sense of what was happening, Royce came running into the kitchens.

"My lady, the west wall has fallen. I am to take you to your chamber."

She'd been trying to prepare for this. In fact, Charlotte thought she would fall to pieces when the wall fell. Instead she found a strange calm settled over her.

"Mrs. Benton, have all the women and children bolt themselves in the solar and the chambers." She followed the man up to the chamber.

"Two men will be posted outside the door. Henry will be here shortly."

The waiting was the worst. Charlotte could see what was happening from the window. And she worried Lord Hallsey would send the bulk of his men across the moat and through the gap in the wall. Were the other walls still under guard? What about the front gate? If they found a way to replace the bridge, all would be lost.

Henry said they would likely bring planks with them to make their own bridge, though she knew Henry would set fire to theirs before letting them make use of it. With no one at the top of the wall to shoot at them, they would have plenty of time. Just as she'd made up her mind to go down and make sure the gates were being guarded, the door opened. Henry strode in and she ran to him, throwing herself in his arms.

"How bad is it?"

Henry's face was grave. "The wall has fallen. Timothy had men loyal to him guarding the wall. During the night, they put up a makeshift bridge." He wiped his brow, and she could see blood spattered across his tunic.

"We are overrun. All is lost." He took her in his arms, kissing her as if it was the last time they would ever see each other.

Charlotte's heart shattered.

"Lock yourself in the chamber. If I die, remember you are the lady of the castle. Lady Ravenskirk."

"Don't say such things. It's going to be fine. Won't the army be here soon?"

"They have not arrived, and I fear 'tis too late. When it's over, only then unbar the door and come out. Demand to be taken to the king. They will not harm you. Not even Lord Hallsey would be so bold. My brothers will come to court to aid you. I am certain your sister's husband's will as well. You will not die."

"Please don't say such things. It's taken me my whole life to find you. I can't lose you now."

"I will find you in the next life." Henry turned to go. Charlotte grabbed him, afraid if he walked out the door she'd never see him again.

"Stay with me awhile?"

"Aye, my love." He stroked her hair. "If I ever find the old woman in the wood again, in this life or the next, I will thank her. She was right about everything. While I would not call Timothy friend, the men who turned against me to fight with him were my men."

Charlotte felt hope bloom in her heart. "But she also said *when you see nothing but darkness ahead, look to the east.* We have to believe the armies will reach us in time."

Henry shook his head. "I think it's the only thing she was wrong about. You have not been outside; you have not seen —so much death. I could not protect my people. My men. I will give my last breath to protect you."

"You did everything possible to protect us all. I can't believe it will end like this. Not after I've come so far."

"I would give all that I have for one more day with you. I swear to you, Charlotte, I will wait for you in the next life. I will watch over you and find a way to send you a sign."

He trailed kisses over her face. "For I know there is more to this life than we can see. And that gives me hope. I will love you even through death."

Henry finished dressing. "I have tarried long enough. I cannot leave the men to fight without me." He held her tight.

"Swear to me you will lock the door when I leave. Remember what I told you."

Charlotte let the tears fall, unable to stop them. She couldn't accept that she would have so little time with Henry. Came all this way, found out her sisters were here, and were on their way, only to have everything ripped away. She didn't believe Henry. Every action Lord Hallsey had taken against him told her he would kill her—if he didn't do something worse. She had to accept she might die without seeing her sisters again. But at least she knew they had made a life here. And she hoped with all her heart they had found happiness and love, as she had.

As Henry walked to the door, he paused. He crossed the room in three strides and pulled her close, raining kisses on her face.

"Now that you know what will happen, if you had the choice, would you have remained in the future?"

She wept as she tried to get the words out.

"Every choice I made has led me to you. I would make every single choice again even knowing today may be our last day on this earth. I love you with all my heart and soul."

She looked her amazing husband in the eye. "Now go out there and kill as many of them as you can."

Chapter Forty-One

Charlotte didn't sleep at all that night. She remained at the window, only turning away to eat and drink when food was brought to her. The interior of the castle had not yet been breached. The men guarding her grew graver and graver every time she opened the door. She urged them to leave, to go out and help Henry. To fight. But the man shook his head.

"Nay, lady. I am charged with protecting you, and I will do so to the last breath."

The fighting being over for the night brought the sounds of men dying to the chamber. Charlotte could hear women crying—and the smell. The smell was unbearable. She knew they were burning the dead so infection wouldn't spread. It was a horrific scene out of a movie, only it wasn't a movie. It was her life.

Charlotte must've fallen asleep, for when she woke it was dawn. And the sounds of battle filled the air. By the way the sun looked, she judged it to be midmorning when she heard a different sound. It sent her running to the window. In the distance she saw bright colors. And Charlotte started screaming. Jumping up and down. The door opened and the men rushed in.

"What is amiss, lady?"

The younger man had a hand on the hilt of his sword. "We heard you screaming."

She pointed to the window. "Look! The army is here."

Both men looked out the window, and she felt the change in the air. She'd never believed you could feel help, but she swore she could.

"Go. Find Henry and fight with him. The tide has turned and we will prevail."

They hesitated. Charlotte pleaded, "I beseech you to go and fight with Henry. Do not let my husband die. Protect him. This is my order as your lady."

Finally they gave her a stiff nod as they left the room. She barred the door behind them and waited. She washed and changed clothes and made a list in her head. There would be bandages, hot water, and herbs needed for the injured. Not to mention the aftermath and cleanup. But she wouldn't complain. Because it would mean she were still alive.

Please keep Henry safe.

She could hear the change in the sounds of battle. And looking out the window, she was in awe of the number of men she saw.

The battle raged. Charlotte paced. Every once in a while she caught a glimpse of Henry. He seemed to be covered from head to toe in blood and muck, and she hoped he was unharmed. She felt helpless here in the tower but knew he would worry about her if she came down. And she didn't want anything to distract him. He needed his full wits about him. To be completely focused on winning.

There was a pounding at the door. "Who's there?"

"I am to tell you *Mellie says hello.*" The voice sounded puzzled as it relayed the message. But Charlotte grinned as she opened the door.

"Oh, it's you."

In front of her stood the piper. The same piper she had seen when she was with the history buffs and in London. The same man whose voice she'd heard when the man chasing her tried to kill her. She swore he'd saved her life.

"My lady, we have not met. I would remember."

"My mistake. You look like someone I met in London."

"I told your sister I would stay with you until the battle is over. My lord, Edward, sent me to watch over you."

She handed him a cup of wine. "Tell me what you know."

He sat down and told her everything that had happened since they'd received the message she and Henry needed help. She was grateful to the man, for he was a natural-born storyteller, and he almost allowed her to take her mind off what was happening outside the window.

They'd talked for several hours when she heard sounds of a fight outside the door. Charlotte had been so shocked to see the piper in the flesh that she had not barred the door behind him. Talk about a stupid mistake.

The door flew open and two men rushed in. The big one swung his sword at the piper's head.

"Get down!"

The man dropped to the floor, and Charlotte grabbed the knife off the desk. She threw it at the man. It was pure luck she caught him in the gut.

There stood the man she hated almost as much as Hallsey. "You. You betrayed my husband."

Timothy looked completely deranged. He was battered, bruised, and bleeding from several cuts. She wondered how he could still be alive. The man with him was scary looking and absolutely huge as he held his gut and cursed.

"Die, demon, die," Timothy shouted as he raised a bow and arrow. Everything happened in slow motion. Charlotte watched as he pulled back his arm and the arrow took flight, and she stood still. Rooted to the spot, unable to move as the arrow came straight for her heart. As she watched, the piper pulled a knife from his boot and threw it, hitting the big, scary man in the throat. He went down with a gurgle. And somehow, the piper still managed to throw himself in front of her at the last moment. The arrow struck him in the heart. He fell to the floor and Charlotte screamed.

Timothy nocked another arrow and came toward her. Charlotte reached down and pulled the second knife from the piper's boot. She didn't know how she did it, but as Timothy got close to her, she lunged forward and thrust upward. He grabbed hold of her; she pulled out the knife and struck again. This time she nailed him in the eye. Her stomach heaved, and Charlotte tried not to throw up as he fell to the floor. She turned and knelt down by the piper.

"You saved my life. I am so sorry. It was my fault for not

locking the door."

He smiled at her. "You, lady, are a warrior in your own right. You saved me from losing my head. I will play for the Thornton women until the end of time." He coughed and blood trickled out of his mouth. She could hear a rattle in his chest as he whispered, "I swear, I will warn them in times of danger. Throughout time."

As he passed, Charlotte reached up and closed his eyes. She was blinded by tears, incredibly grateful he had given his own life to save her.

"I swear, I will live the rest of my days being happy and filled with hope." She made a decision. She could tell the battle was at an end, and she needed Henry. Only he would understand what she had been through.

Chapter Forty-Two

The next week had been difficult. The army routed Hallsey and his men. She found out later Lord Hallsey had been killed by an arrow. So many men lost their lives. From knights to peasants, death did not discriminate.

Charlotte met Henry's brothers. She found them all good-looking and charming. Her only wish was to have met them for the first time under better circumstances.

When she met James and William, she could understand why her sisters had married them. They promised to take her back to Falconburg to see them both. She still couldn't believe Melinda was pregnant and due in a week or two. And, of course, William wouldn't bring Lucy to a battle. They were anxiously waiting for her. And Charlotte was looking forward to finally making the journey.

The new priest was doing well, and busy with the aftermath of the battle. Edward had been saddened by the loss of his favorite piper.

"I'd like to have a statue commissioned and put in the

garden. He saved my life, and I would like to remember him always."

Edward looked touched. "I thank you."

"He said he would watch over the Thornton women for all time. Warn them of any impending danger." She smiled. "I can't be the only Thornton woman. Perhaps it is time for you and your brothers to marry?"

Henry burst out laughing. "Look at the horror upon his face."

Edward struck him, and then they were rolling in the dirt like two small children. Robert and Christian called out helpful suggestions and insults.

Charlotte laughed in what felt like the first time in years.

The swordsmith beamed at Henry. "My apologies, my lord, for not having the blades completed sooner." The man held them out, a proud look on his face.

"Fine craftsmanship." He held the blade with the amethyst up to the light. "Charlotte will love them."

Henry was excited to give her the daggers. He went in search of his strong wife. He wanted to give them to her before they left this morning on the journey to visit her sisters. He was looking forward to finally meeting the women he'd heard so much about. Women from the future.

Henry found her standing on the battlements looking out over the land. The sound of rebuilding was all around them. The walls would be repaired and reinforced. With the wind blowing her hair around her face, she looked like a warrior goddess come to life.

He held the daggers behind his back. "I wanted to give these to you after we married, but they weren't completed until today."

She held out her hands to accept the gift. Henry watched her face as she held the first one up, the one with the sapphire in the hilt. As she turned it to the light, he watched her face fall.

Did she not like them? 'Twas stupid to give a woman blades. He should have given her jewelry.

"The soul is here for its own joy." She looked afraid.

In a whisper, she read the inscription on the other blade. The one with amethyst in the hilt. "Om. The sound of the universe smiling."

His wife looked around and it was as if she thought someone was coming for her. Henry tensed, his hand going to the hilt of his sword.

The moment passed. She exhaled and looked around. Her face brightened.

"I love them. They are beautiful." She slid the first blade into her boot. As she reached down to put the second blade in her boot, her finger touched the point. Three crimson dots appeared.

"You cut yourself." Before his eyes, Charlotte began to fade. Henry heard the sound of metal screaming, voices buzzing all around them, and lightning tore through the sky.

With complete certainty, he knew she was going back to her own time. Henry lunged forward.

"She is mine. Charlotte belongs here with me. I will not let her go."

The sky seemed to tear in two as they fell.

Charlotte came to gasping. There was a heavy weight on top of her, and she was finding it hard to breathe. She shoved at the lump. It was her husband.

She looked around, taking in the details. Charlotte's eyes filled with tears.

"You pulled me back."

Henry blinked several times and sat up, his hands on his head.

"What happened? You cut yourself on the blade and you began to fade. I could see through you to the wall and the fields beyond. There was a most fearsome noise, and I knew I would lose you. I reached out and pulled you to me." He gathered her in his arms. "I prevented you from going back to your own time. Are you angry?"

"My place is here. With you. My sisters are here." She stroked his face. "Right here. Right now. This is my time. This is my present."

She tried to explain to him what had happened, and Henry looked around to see if anyone else had noticed. Surely they would think her a faerie if they saw her disappear in front of their eyes.

"I heard a voice. It was Aunt Pittypat. She told me to trust my heart, trust in my love for you. By doing so, it would hold me where I was meant to be."

Charlotte reached out a hand to Henry. "Let's go. I want to talk to my sisters about what happened. See if they had a similar experience."

"You are a remarkable woman, Charlotte Merriweather Thornton."

Chapter Forty-Three

It took them three long days to travel to Falconburg Castle. Charlotte was counting down the minutes until she'd finally be reunited with her sisters.

"My sisters used to want to shoot me when I asked, 'Are we there yet?'"

William and James laughed. "When we cross the next hill, you'll see Falconburg," James said.

She was content to listen to Henry talk with them as they traveled. Charlotte had been so lost in her thoughts she hadn't been paying attention. When she looked up, there was the castle.

"Wow. That's impressive." She looked at Henry and blew him a kiss. "But not as impressive as Ravenskirk."

As they rode into the courtyard, Charlotte practically jumped off the horse. The doors to the castle opened and Lucy ran out. She paused, kissed William on the mouth, then ran to Charlotte, throwing herself in her arms.

She was laughing and crying at the same time. "I can't

believe you're here. You don't know how much I've missed you."

Charlotte couldn't believe her eyes. "Your hair is gray!"

"Right. It must be a shock. You have the same look Melinda did."

"I don't understand. Why do you look so different?"

At that point, Melinda waddled down the steps and Charlotte clapped a hand over her mouth.

"You're huge!"

"I'm due any day. Good to see you too, brat. And Lucy looks different because she came through in the year 1307."

"You've been here *twenty-three* years?" Charlotte turned to Melinda. "Other than being ready to explode, you look the same. How long have you been here?"

"Three years. It was 1327 when I came through. When we heard you were here, we tried to figure out how long you've been in the past."

"Only since the end of May. I left in May of 2016."

"What?"

James interrupted them. "My darling wife, there are many ears—why don't you come into the solar and talk there."

Melinda kissed him on the lips. "Thank you for bringing my sister home. We'll go inside." She turned and looked at Henry.

"You must be Lord Ravenskirk. I'd recognize that hair and those eyes anywhere. You Thornton brothers all look alike. I don't know how to thank you for rescuing Charlotte."

Lucy added, "I hear congratulations are in order."

Charlotte started to laugh. "Wait until you hear the tale. Poor Henry. He was forced to marry me."

William snorted. "The Thornton brothers are all stubborn. None of them will do anything against their will."

Henry arched a brow. "I hear you know my brother Edward. He is much more stubborn than I. Though I hear you are good with the blade. Care to meet me in the lists?"

James smirked. "And me. We'll let the women talk while we see what you're made of, whelp."

Melinda rolled her eyes. "Come on, they'll be out here all afternoon."

Charlotte looked at Melinda's home as they walked through the hall. It was a beautiful castle, and she could see Melinda's touch everywhere she looked.

"You know, if you wouldn't have said you didn't have a third sister, we might have avoided the whole almost-dying thing."

Lucy spoke first. "I'm sorry, sis. We were being careful. Both of us have been accused of being witches."

"If we said we had a sister and no one ever met her, it would raise suspicion," Mellie added. "We never dreamt it would cause so many problems."

"At the time it seemed like a good idea." Lucy hugged Charlotte. "We're so glad you're here and we're all together again."

Melinda led them into the light-filled solar. She sat down with a groan. "My feet are killing me."

A woman brought in wine and cookies.

"Are those sugar cookies?" Charlotte picked up two.

Lucy laughed. "We both like to bake. Wait until Henry finds out how much we spend on spices. He'll hide his gold from you."

"I have my own gold. I brought gems and coins with me."

Melinda leaned forward. "Did you get our message?"

"What message?"

Lucy rolled her eyes. "We wrote a note, put it in a bottle, sealed it up, and put it behind a stone at Blackford. With your initials on it. To be sure you would find it."

"I never made it to Blackford. When I decided to try and find you both, I thought I'd go to Falconburg first. Start at the most recent scene. Only I never made it there." Both her sisters leaned forward, and Charlotte filled them in on everything that had happened since Melinda disappeared.

"When I get back, I'll destroy the bottle. Don't want some stranger finding it in the future and causing problems." Lucy grinned. "You think Henry's stubborn? Wait until I tell you about William."

"I still can't believe Simon went to so much trouble to see all of us dead. Talk about a Grade A bastard." Lucy rolled her eyes.

"If he hadn't, we might not all be here," Charlotte said. They were all silent for a few moments thinking about what that meant.

"I can't believe you came back and only three years after me," Melinda said. "I wonder if it's because it was close to midsummer? I came through in February and Lucy came through in summer, like you."

Lucy added, "Let's not forget the raven. And the blood."

"And the objects." Charlotte pulled out the daggers from her boots. She handed one to each sister.

Melinda and Lucy said at the same time, "It's the same inscription as your tattoos."

Charlotte nodded. "It was right before we came here. Henry gifted these to me. He'd seen my tattoos and thought I would like the inscriptions on the daggers. I put one in my boot, and when I slid the other one in, it slipped and nicked my finger. That's when everything went haywire."

Lucy and Melinda both started talking over each other. "Did the lights turn rainbow?"

"Did you hear the sound of metal ripping?"

"All of that. And I heard Aunt Pittypat talking to me."

Melinda tapped her chin. "So it seems like one of the first days of the season, our blood, some kind of object, and that huge raven. All of those things have to be in place for us to travel through time."

"And don't forget the storm." Lucy shuddered. "It was terrible."

"I know. Lightning struck the car and I thought for sure I was dead," Charlotte said.

Lucy grinned. "I still can't believe you stole a car and crashed it into the ocean!"

Melinda tapped her chin. "I know you'll both think I'm crazy, but I've given it a lot of thought. I think the raven is some kind of reincarnation of Aunt Pittypat."

Charlotte thought she must have the same stunned look on her face as Lucy. She slowly nodded.

"I felt like she was with me a lot of the time. It would make sense. She would've loved the adventure."

Lucy ate a cookie. "Let's hope the Merriweather curses are finally broken. No more bad judgment in men..." Her voice trailed off. "Though I don't know about both of you, but my sense of direction is still as bad as it ever was."

They both laughed. "Mine too," Melinda said. "You know the trouble I had when I arrived."

"Luckily I met Henry right away, so I didn't have to try to find my way," Charlotte said.

They talked for a while, and Melinda said, "What did you do about the house?"

"I gave it to Jake. He's done so much for all of us, I thought it was for the best." Charlotte ate another cookie. "These are so good. You're going to have to show me how you make them here."

She took a sip of wine. "I took all the money we had left and exchanged it into gems and gold coins. I wasn't sure what I would need when I got here." She smiled at her sisters. "Though I found my very own knight and I haven't spent a cent of it. I'd be happy to share with you both."

Lucy laughed. "I think all of our husbands are rich."

"Keep it," Melinda said. "But what if you couldn't have come back in time?"

"I put plans in place. Jake wouldn't get the house until I was declared dead. And I figured I could always resell the gems and the coins."

"I wish I'd had time to spend with history buffs before I got here."

"Did you bring the recipes with you?" Lucy looked hopeful. "There are a couple of Aunt Pittypat's I've been dying to make, but I can't remember exactly how she made some of them."

Charlotte nodded. "I wrote down the important ones in a journal, along with bits and pieces I thought would be useful. It's in my trunk. I'll get it now if you want."

Melinda waved her down. "No, sit. There'll be plenty of time for that later."

Charlotte took a deep breath. "I'm really sorry, you guys. I didn't believe you, Mellie. When you vanished and the authorities said you committed suicide, I knew. You're too stubborn to kill yourself."

"Pot. Meet kettle."

"I'm so glad we're all together again. As long as we're together, everything will be all right." Lucy wiped a tear from her eye.

Charlotte patted her on the shoulder. "It was Memorial weekend when I left for England. Remember the crowds? The heat?"

They reminisced about home and the beach. All the things they missed. Melinda rubbed her back. "Tell us you brought chocolate and music."

Charlotte shook her head. "I was afraid to bring back any

kind of electronics. And as to chocolate, I figured why torture myself? As soon as I ate it, the stuff would be gone with no way to make more."

Both sisters groaned, and Lucy said, "We were somehow hoping you'd have a stash we could raid."

"After what you both told me about almost drowning or being burnt at the stake, I'm glad I didn't bring back anything incriminating. I had a hard enough time. You know, I almost forgot to tell you what the gypsy, Marielle, told me." Charlotte leaned forward in her seat. She said, *"You will find your sisters in England. But not this England."*

"I've got chills." Lucy rubbed her arms.

"She also told me to look out for danger. Can you believe she knew about your unicorn necklace, Mellie? I'm so sorry I lost it down the well."

"It doesn't matter. I'm just glad it found its way to you." Melinda looked like she wanted to say more, but Charlotte wouldn't pry. They had plenty of time to be with each other. The rest of their lives.

Chapter Forty-Four

Epilogue

One Year Later

Melinda held Emma Pittypat Rivers on her lap. The door opened and a messenger staggered in. James took the message and called for the healer. Two of his knights took the man to the kitchen. James read the missive, his face turning a grayish color. Alarm spread through her.

"Call William and Henry in from the lists."

Melinda took Emma and put the sleeping baby in a cradle so she wouldn't wake and start crying. "What's happened?"

"I must speak with Henry."

"I am here," Henry said as he strode into the room, the rest following behind him.

James looked grim. "You should sit."

Melinda looked at him, and some kind of unspoken

message seemed to pass between them. She was glad both her sisters were spending the summer at Falconburg.

"I swore I would never breathe a word. He didn't want you to go around stirring up trouble."

Henry looked confused. "What the bloody hell are you on about?"

"'Tis your brother. John."

"John is dead."

James shook his head. "Nay. He is alive. John is the infamous bandit in the woods. He has been betrayed. Your brother is imprisoned in the tower, awaiting death."

Books by Cynthia Luhrs
Listed in the correct reading order

THRILLER
There Was A Little Girl - coming soon!

THORNTON BROTHERS TIME TRAVEL
Darkest Knight

MERRIWEATHER SISTERS TIME TRAVEL
A Knight to Remember
Knight Moves
Lonely is the Knight

THE SHADOW WALKER GHOST SERIES
Lost in Shadow
Desired by Shadow
Iced in Shadow
Reborn in Shadow
Born in Shadow
Embraced by Shadow

A JIG THE PIG ADVENTURE

(Children's Picture Books)
Beware the Woods
I am NOT a Chicken!

Want More?

Thank you for reading my book. If you enjoyed it, please consider writing a few words in a review to help others discover the Merriweather books. Let me know your thoughts. I love to hear from my readers. To find out when there's a new book release, please visit my website http://cluhrs.com/ and sign up for my newsletter. Want to drop me a line? Please LIKE my page on Facebook. Love connecting with all of my readers because without you, none of this would be possible. http://www.facebook.com/cynthialuhrsauthor

P.S. Prefer another form of social media? You'll find links to all my social media sites there.

Thank you!

Mailing List

Subscribe to Cynthia's Mailing List http://cluhrs.com/connect/ to receive exclusive updates from Cynthia Luhrs and to be the first to get instant access to cover releases, chapter excerpts, and win great prizes!

About the Author

Cynthia Luhrs is the author of the ghostly Shadow Walker novels and the Merriweather Sisters Time Travel Romance novels set in medieval England. Her idea of a perfect day is no interruptions and the freedom to live in her head all day, writing to her heart's content, a glass of sweet tea next to her as she creates the next book. Of course her tiger cats frequently disrupt this oasis of serenity.

Made in the USA
Middletown, DE
13 October 2016